"You can't seriously think I'd be so trite as to ask you up to my loft to see my etchings. I want to show you the real thing, the originals," Jacques whispered. His face was very close to her and his breath lay warm on her cheek.

Vanessa arched her body to his in unconscious desire to be as close to him as possible, to become a part of him. His large hands stroked the smooth curves of her body, lingering on the fullness of her breasts, descending slowly to her stomach, and coming to rest between her thighs. Instinctively she twisted her fingers in his wiry red hair and pulled his head closer to her.

They hesitated for another moment, looking deeply into each other's eyes, knowing that the pain of waiting just a small moment longer would intensify the ultimate pleasure of their union. . . .

Dear Reader,

It is our pleasure to bring you a new experience in reading that goes beyond category writing. The settings of **Harlequin American Romance** give a sense of place and culture that is uniquely American, and the characters are warm and believable. The stories are of "today" and have been chosen to give variety within the vast scope of romance fiction.

The sensitivity and the expertise of a chromist are found in the character of Vanessa VanderPoel, the heroine of *Canvas of Passion*. The slick, cool talent of Jacques Powers, the modernist painter, will intrigue you and hold you spellbound. From Manhattan to Connecticut to the white tile roof condos of Las Hadas, Mexico, Deirdre Mardon's first novel shows a rare talent.

From the early days of Harlequin, our primary concern has been to bring you novels of the highest quality. **Harlequin American Romance** is no exception. Enjoy!

Vivian Stephens

Vivian Stephens
Editorial Director
Harlequin American Romance
919 Third Avenue,
New York, N.Y. 10022

Canvas of Passion

DEIRDRE MARDON

Harlequin Books

TORONTO • NEW YORK • LOS ANGELES • LONDON
AMSTERDAM • PARIS • SYDNEY • HAMBURG
STOCKHOLM • ATHENS • TOKYO • MILAN

Published June 1983

First printing April 1983

ISBN 0-373-16009-7

Chapter One

"The boss wants to see you, sweetie."

Maynard placed a cup of hot coffee on the desk in front of Vanessa. He unfolded a paper napkin and smoothed it carefully before removing the plastic top that covered the cup. "Big doings today," he announced in a cultivated voice.

"What's going on?" Vanessa looked up to ask.

"You'll see. Bauman wants to see you in his office right away." He rolled his eyes upward and gave her an enigmatic look before turning and slipping out of her glass-walled office, leaving the door open behind him. She watched his graceful body thread its way through the narrow aisle between the presses. "Maynard!" she called after him to thank him for bringing her morning coffee, but the rumble of the presses drowned out the words she had planned to say to his retreating back. The third large press had just started up for the day's run.

Vanessa sighed as she stood and smoothed her wool skirt. She hated mornings that began with a session in Bauman's office. She replaced the top on the coffee, hoping it would still be warm when she returned to her office. She traced Maynard's steps through the pounding pressroom and passed into a fluorescent-lit corridor that led to a wooden door on which a brass plaque read "Richard Bauman, President, Columbia Atelier." Knocking quietly, she entered the office without awaiting his reply. She stepped into a thick beige carpet, which muffled the sounds of the atelier, and quickly shut the door behind her to drown out the clamor of the machines.

Richard Bauman stood up behind a wide desk of glass and chrome. He nodded in her direction.

"This is Vanessa VanderPoel, my best chromist. She'll be assisting you with your prints."

Vanessa glanced at the man seated in a chair to the right of Bauman's desk. The stranger had not bothered to rise at her entrance, nor did he now. She strained in vain to hear the mumbled words that acknowledged the introduction.

"Vanessa, this is Jacques Power. He is going to be doing a series of abstract prints with us. Columbia is honored to be working with Jacques. These will be his first prints." Bauman was actually rubbing his hands together nervously.

She stared at the stranger's bright red hair with what she hoped was an expressionless face. Jacques Power... *the* Jacques Power. So, this is what the renowned abstract painter looked like. "The young tiger," she had heard him called within New York's usually catty art world. "A legend in his own time," and, she narrowed her eyes as she recalled another label— "Jacques the Terrible." If his famous temper was anything like that surprising red hair— Well, heaven help them all at the atelier. And, he was rude as well, she noted silently. His long legs were stretched before him and crossed languorously at the ankles. He wore scuffed leather boots with white lines where the salt on the winter streets had marked them. His costume consisted of a blue work shirt and denim jeans, both faded almost to white except where blotches of paint stained the knees of his pants and the cuffs of his shirt. On his face, beneath the sprinkling of freckles that matched his rumpled and wiry red hair, he wore an expression of jaded boredom.

"Nice to meet you, Mr. Power. I'll be happy to assist you in any way I am able," Vanessa said politely.

"What does she mean—assist me? I never use assistants." He spoke to Bauman, not once glancing in Vanessa's direction. His words were brusque.

"You know, Jacques, separating the colors for the prints. Most artists don't do their own—it's too time consuming." Bauman, who was still standing, came to the front of his desk and put an arm around Vanessa's shoulder. "She's the best. She's done prints for Erté, Neiman, Dali—you name it. They all love her work and you will too. We're lucky to have her here at Columbia."

Vanessa was surprised at the unctuous tone of her employer's voice. He must need the contract with Power badly, she assumed. She noted a fine line of perspiration on Bauman's upper lip. Obviously, he was thrilled to have Power doing his prints at the atelier. His attitude seemed to confirm the rumors that had been making the rounds in art circles—that Columbia was in deep financial trouble. Bauman must have been out a hefty advance to sign up the high-priced Jacques Power to put together a print package at Columbia. She gazed at the redhead through lowered lids. His youth surprised her. He could not be more than forty.

"I won't be needing her," said Power with no effort to soften the blow. "I always do all my own work."

"But, Jacques, almost everyone uses a chromist. It's extremely technical—"

"Not me. Nobody screws around with my work." The tone of his voice was final. A silence followed. Bauman rubbed his hands together in distress. He gave Vanessa a pleading look.

"Why don't you get yourself a cup of coffee, dear? Jacques and I have some things to talk about."

"Certainly, Richard. Nice meeting you, Mr. Power," she recited evenly, although her teeth were clenched. She gave him a tight, mechanical smile and turned to leave the office.

"Get me one with cream and sugar," said Power.

"Pardon me?" She turned to face the sprawling artist.

"Cream and sugar. And a buttered roll," he added.

She felt a surge of anger stab her in the pit of the stomach and travel like an electric current to the top of her head. Her ice-blue eyes locked with the hazel ones of Jacques Power. From the corner of her eye she was aware that Richard Bauman was breathing heavily and was actually wringing his hands. Bauman cleared his throat nervously in the charged silence.

After another heartbeat, Vanessa said, "Sorry, Jacques, you've got the wrong cookie. I'm the chromist, not the gofer." She turned back to the heavy wooden door and threw it open, letting in the cacophony of the pressroom. From past encounters with Bauman, she knew it was futile to slam his door with any effect, so she closed it softly behind her. She stood for a moment on the other side of the door, allowing the anger to wash over her in crimson waves.

"Of all the conceited egomaniacs! Of all the...the unspeakably rude...the...the...." Words strong enough to expel the anger eluded her and the red haze swimming before her pupils pushed all coherent thoughts from her head. The disrespect implicit in his posture was bad enough, but she had seen what Bauman most certainly had not: Power was laughing at her. She had seen the weathered lines around his gold-flecked hazel eyes crinkle in amusement when he realized he had hit one of her buttons.

"Well, tough!" she mumbled under her breath. "He doesn't need a chromist—I certainly don't need another neurotic, self-obsessed artist to deal with! I wouldn't touch his prints with a ten-foot pole!"

She returned to the end of the corridor and stopped to compose herself before entering the pressroom. Taking a deep breath and holding her chin high, she threaded her way through the narrow space between the thundering machines. A series of wolf whistles followed her progress. It was almost a game the men who ran the presses at the atelier engaged in with her. Vanessa suffered from a distressing tendency to blush under strain, which the pressmen had discovered eight years previously when she came to work at Columbia Atelier, fresh out of art school. At least twice a week since then, they had given her the wolf-whistle treatment, although she had long since ceased to blush at their noisy attentions. Today, however, she was painfully aware that her cheeks were aflame even before she entered their brightly lit workroom. Vinnie, the foreman, whistled longest and loudest as she crossed quickly to the relative sanctuary of her glass-walled office.

The coffee was still hot and she gratefully uncapped it and sipped it pensively. Her heartbeat had returned to normal by the time Maynard knocked at the door of her office.

"How'd it go, sweetie?" He entered and shut the door behind him.

"I suppose you might call it an unmitigated disaster, Maynard." She leaned her chin on one hand and gazed up at him when he perched his lithe body on a corner of her desk. "He has Jacques Power in there with him. *The* Jacques Power."

"Aha! That's who we thought it was. The red hair, you know." He patted the back of her free hand where it lay on the desk. "And Power chewed you up and spat you out—already?"

"I'm not sure it was quite that bad. He certainly was rude enough, though. And I mean rude! He told me to get him coffee and a buttered roll. He said he doesn't want a chromist 'screwing around' with his work. Those are his exact words. He doesn't want help from anyone."

Vanessa began to relax in the warmth of Maynard's sympathetic presence. He clucked at all the appropriate places as she related the story of her visit to Bauman's office. Maynard was her best friend at the atelier, indeed in all of New York City. With him she could let down the icily aristocratic manner she seemed to project to people who did not know her well. Maynard had a reputation for being "bitchy," but he had never shown that side of himself to Vanessa. Within the confines of her office or in his fussily decorated small Park Avenue apartment where they had shared many dinners together, they were able to be themselves.

"I saw him coming out of the elevator this morning. He's very sexy."

"Sexy!" she sputtered. "He looks like he's never brushed that hair of his and like he lives in those jeans! Besides, he's not my type at all."

"Oh? And who *is* your type?" he asked her quietly.

"I—I don't know. Someone like Andrew, I suppose."

"You don't want another Andrew, do you?"

"You're right, Maynard. One Andrew was enough for me and I couldn't live through the pain of another man like him. I want a man who needs people, who needs *me*. Andrew didn't need me and I couldn't help him. I only wish I could have," she said wistfully.

"Nobody could help Andrew, sweetie. Nobody."

"But I tried. I would have done anything for him, but he wouldn't let me." Vanessa looked away at an invisible spot on the wall. She and Maynard had been through the same discussion about her dead husband many times before. It usually ended with Vanessa sniffing daintily, throwing back her streaked brown hair, and announcing in a mock-British accent, "But life goes on and the living with it."

"'Death is the only pure, beautiful conclusion of a great passion,'" recited Maynard.

"Who said that?"

"D. H. Lawrence."

"You always have a nice quotation, Maynard, but I really wouldn't call that one appropriate," admitted Vanessa.

"Why not? It's so romantic," he said.

"Because by the time Andrew died he had been totally depressed for so long that no one could get to him. There *was* no great passion. There was nothing left of him but the shell of the man I had married. I used to think everything had been *my* fault, but his doctor convinced me afterward that people who are that seriously depressed make everyone around them feel guilty before they can admit to themselves that *they* are their own illness. He made me feel better, but that was later...after the accident. After Andrew was gone." She swallowed hard.

"I think you're still in love with him, sweetie."

"No, I'm not, Maynard. I almost never think of him except when you and I get into these discussions. Perhaps I may still be in love with the idea of what might have been. But certainly not with who he really was when he died. It was horrible, just watching him get worse and worse and being unable to help him. But life was much more painful for him, we can be sure.

"Anyway, Andrew is the distant past. He's been dead for three—well, it will be three years at Christmas. And I have totally remade my life."

"And *I* still believe Lawrence's sentiments are lovely ones," said Maynard with a change-the-topic tone.

"Yes, you are an old romantic hiding under your guise of cynicism." She laughed.

"Don't tell anyone, do you hear? I'd rather be known as a worldly cynic!" His eyes twinkled.

"Get out of here, Maynard. I have to get to work. I have two prints to do." She tossed her long hair back in a gesture of friendly dismissal.

"But what about Power's prints? Aren't you going to do those?"

"I wouldn't touch them on a bet. Not that he'd have me," she added quickly.

"Oh, come on, he'll be begging for you before long. Just wait until he tries to take one of those abstract drawings of his apart for the first time," said Maynard confidently, patting her hand once more.

"I doubt it. Not the famous Jacques Power." Vanessa stood and removed a pale blue smock from a peg on the wall behind her desk. She put on the smock, buttoning it over the heather-colored cashmere sweater she wore over a matching wool skirt. The pale blue exactly mirrored the ice blue of her eyes.

"Yes, famous. Also... well, watch out for him, my dear. He's known as a womanizer."

"I told you, he's not my type. He's not the slightest bit attractive to me."

"Fame is a powerful aphrodisiac," warned Maynard.

"Don't worry about *me*, Maynard. *You* watch out for him," she returned with a grin.

"'I'm tired of Love, I'm still more tired of Rhyme. But Money gives me pleasure all the time.' Anyway, I'm not exactly *his* type, I think that's obvious by looking at him. Ta-ta, sweetie. Back to the salt mines."

Vanessa was already removing a sketch from one of the wide drawers of the print cabinet behind her desk as Maynard left the office. She began to separate the first color of a fourteen-color landscape the atelier had contracted to print for the estate of a renowned French painter. She was totally absorbed in her work when a soft knock on the door caused her to raise her head. Richard Bauman stood outside the door awaiting her permission to enter. *He wants a favor,* she said to herself as she nodded her head at him. In other circumstances, Bauman would have barged into her office without knocking.

"Vanessa, I'm so sorry about this morning."

"Sorry about what, Richard? I didn't notice anything," she lied.

"Power. He was unbearable to you. He just doesn't know about chromists. He's never done prints before— he's strictly a painter. You've seen his work, I'm sure."

"So?"

"So, I hope you won't hold the things he said against him."

"Why should I? I don't expect I'll have occasion to be speaking to him again."

"Don't be like that. He's important to me. To Columbia. We've got to get a perfect set of prints. It just *has* to go right." Bauman's voice vibrated with urgency.

"How does that affect me, Richard? He won't be using a chromist anyway. He told us so himself. Quite clearly, I thought."

"Yes, I know what he said, but he doesn't realize what he's talking about. You'll see, he'll be needing you before long. I know he's—shall we say—'difficult.' But he's an extremely important artist, one of the greatest coups we have ever landed at Columbia. He's never done lithographs before. These will be the first on the market. Can you imagine the demand for them? No one can afford to buy his paintings anymore. The public will be mad to get their hands on his prints."

"That has nothing to do with me, Richard. Get someone else to separate his colors if he needs help, someone who'll go out for his coffee and buttered rolls. I am fully occupied this week, as it is. I'm doing the estate prints now and have two tax-shelter portfolios that must be finished before the end of December, as you well know." She was firm and cool, determined to end the discussion.

"Vanessa, I really need this business." Bauman hesitated as if deciding how much he should say. Something told him to go on. "Things aren't going well for me financially. I need your cooperation. You are the best in the business. No one can touch the fine quality of your work. Please say you'll help me out."

Vanessa felt a stab of compassion for the nervous

and supplicant man looking down at her. Bauman had been good to her over the years. He had hired her and trained her directly out of art school. He had been patient and made few demands on her as she traveled the labyrinthine path of illness with Andrew. He had even given her a month off, with pay, after the automobile accident that had claimed Andrew's life and widowed her at twenty-six.

"All right, Richard," she assented with a sigh. "*If* he asks. He probably won't, though. He's pretty independent. But you will have to tell Power that a chromist is not a gofer. No coffee errands."

"I will, I will," he answered, grabbing her hand and kissing it. "I'll tell him you're the highest-paid chromist we've ever had at Columbia. The best!"

"That'll really impress him, Richard," she answered drily. "He gets more for one canvas than I earn in a year."

"You want more money? You want a raise?"

"No, Richard, I don't want more money. I have all I need right now. You've been a good employer to me all this time. I'll be nice to him for you."

"Thank you, Vanessa. I knew you'd see my side of the problem. You have no idea how much I appreciate your cooperation."

"But, Richard, you could do me one favor."

"Anything. What is it? A bigger office? A couple of days off? After New Year's of course," he added quickly. "Tell me what you want!"

"Just don't toady to him so much, please. It's not dignified."

He gave her a funny look. "Am I? Do I toady to

him? How awful." He shifted his eyes away from hers.

"People will think you're really in trouble and you know how quickly word gets around in this business."

"You're right." He rubbed his hands together. "He's just another neurotic artist, no one to be impressed by," he said weakly, as if to convince himself of the fact.

"Right, Richard."

"But—"

"No buts, Richard. You're the owner of one of the most respected ateliers in the entire city. He needs *you*, Richard. Keep telling yourself that."

"Okay, Vanessa, you have a valid point." But his doubtful tone made a lie of his words. She realized that financial troubles at Columbia must be worse than she had suspected. She felt sorry for Richard. She knew his pampered wife spent money faster than he could possibly have made it. The print business was booming, but so were expenses. Labor contracts, rents, even the cost of paper and inks, had escalated astronomically in the past five years. For Bauman's sake she promised herself to be nice to Jacques Power no matter how he provoked her. Well, if not nice, she would try to be tolerant of him.

She smiled a winning smile at Richard and saw him relax visibly. At twenty-nine, her face had lost the roundness of youth and had taken on an aristocratic angularity, which was less beautiful than it was striking. Her light blue eyes, set too far apart for her own taste, were her most noticeable feature. When she smiled as she now did, they softened and warmed the

sometimes haughty appearance she was capable of
presenting. Maynard had convinced her to have the
front of her light brown hair streaked the summer before and she had been pleased with the sophisticated
effect the subtle lightening had produced. At first she
had objected, had shunned the very idea of such arti-
fice, but the difficult circumstances of Andrew's untimely death had caused the unexpected appearance
of prematurely gray hairs. Maynard had argued con-
vincingly that a woman in her late twenties had no
business showing gray hairs to the world unless she
was blessed with a natural, all white streak. He had
accompanied her to the salon of a ridiculously over-
priced stylist on West 57th Street, chattering all the
way uptown in a taxi, afraid no doubt that she would
lose her nerve during the half-hour ride from the atelier at twenty-sixth and Park Avenue South. It became apparent to Vanessa that Raul, the stylist, had
been a social protégé of Maynard's many years before. From the deference he paid to her colleague
upon their arrival at the salon, she suspected that Raul
had met the rich and famous clientele who now fre-
quented his shop through Maynard. The two men had
clucked over Vanessa, fussed with her hair, pulling it
this way and that, until they had agreed—without consulting her—on the best style to enhance the effect of
her high cheekbones and wide-set eyes. Although the
bill for the haircut and streaking had been shockingly
expensive by Vanessa's standards, the stylist had personally and artfully made up her face on the house. At
the time the cosmetics had seemed so exaggerated to
her that she had continued home in a taxi, rather than

hop on the uptown subway for the short ride to her apartment on Seventy-second Street. But, examining the makeup at home later, she admitted to herself that Raul had done wonderful things with her eyes and she had been using some of his tricks, although subtly, ever since.

"Where are you having lunch, Vanessa?" asked Richard.

"I'm just bringing in a sandwich. I want to leave early this afternoon to finish my Christmas shopping, so I don't plan to go out to lunch. Why?"

"I thought you could have lunch with Jacques and kind of explain to him how the process works. You know, so he'll understand better—"

"Come *on*, Richard! Stop trying to get me to play your little games. I won't do it. This is strictly business. I'll do as you ask as far as the prints are concerned, but don't try to make me like him as well."

"All right. It was just a thought. See you later." Bauman left and she returned to the mylar she had been drawing.

Vanessa pressed toward the take-out counter of the lobby deli, impatient to give her lunch order and get out of the steaming shop overflowing with hungry office workers equally eager to order sandwiches.

"One tuna fish, white bread. One provolone, mayo, rye bread. Two black coffees," she called out when at last her turn arrived. The counter man shouted her order over his shoulder and began to fill two containers with coffee.

"Who's the other sandwich for?" asked a low voice close to her ear. "I thought you didn't 'gofer.'"

Startled, she turned her head and found herself a mere six inches from the green eyes of Jacques Power. He was not as tall as he had appeared while seated with his long legs extended in front of him. In fact, in the three-inch heels she wore, she had to tilt her head back only slightly to look directly into his eyes. His wiry thinness had made him seem taller than he actually was, she realized.

"I do not 'gofer,' Mr. Power. This is a favor for someone who frequently does the same for me. Not that it's any of your business, I might add." She turned her head away from the disturbing eyes that seemed to be devouring the features of her face. His eyelashes were so blond they were nearly invisible.

"One of the other girls?"

"We are not 'girls,' Mr. Power. We are women, professional women. There are no 'girls' at the atelier. And no, it's not for one of the women."

"My, my, Miss VanderPoel, aren't we defensive! Your manner is rather off-putting, to say the least. It's no wonder you're still *Miss* VanderPoel at your age. What are you, about thirty?" As he spoke smoothly and lightly she noticed the same crinkles of amusement at the corners of his blond-fringed eyes. She wanted to move away from him, but the crush of people clamoring for service kept her rooted to the spot. She could feel red spots begin to grow on her cheeks and she willed herself to calm her temper, which was beginning to simmer beneath her placid-looking facade.

"Look, Mr. Power, I don't have to—"

"Jacques. The name is Jacques, Vanessa."

"Well, the name is VanderPoel and I don't have anything to say to you," she answered quickly.

"Have I offended you? I don't have the fine manners that you do, Miss VanderPoel, and if I've been rude, you'll just have to forgive me. I didn't enjoy all the advantages of upbringing that you obviously did."

"Yes, we all know about your humble beginnings on the Boston docks, but you've been around long enough to smooth out the rough edges, don't you think? Why don't you simply put a lid on the blue-collar artist image and leave me alone?" She reached for the white paper bag of coffee and sandwiches and began to push her way toward the cashier at the end of the counter. Jacques followed her, making way for her passage through the crowd with his long arms. He wore a honey-colored sheepskin jacket and looked like a cowboy fresh off the range. His red hair glistened under the bright lights of the delicatessen.

"Here, hold this," ordered Vanessa. She thrust the paper bag into his large hands as she reached the cashier. She opened her leather handbag and pulled out a small coin purse to pay for the lunches. Her fingers fumbled for the bills and coins within, disobedient to the orders her brain was sending to them. As she reached for the change the cashier extended, she dropped the small purse and heard the coins it had contained fall to the floor. She saw dimes and subway tokens roll under the feet of the people still standing in line to order sandwiches. She bent to pick up the purse and felt the contents of her open handbag slide out. Everything fell in a heap into a puddle of gritty melting snow and ice on the terrazzo floor. Jacques Power crouched at her side rapidly gathering a tube of lipstick, a compact, and a red leather address book in his long-fingered hands.

"See what you made me do!" she said in exasperation, immediately regretting that she had let the abrasive artist see how he had nonplussed her. She reached for her tortoise comb at the same moment that his fingers touched it and she drew back her arm in shock when her skin brushed against the freckled back of his hand. Her hand burned where his had rubbed against it.

"Never mind, I'll take care of it," she said without daring to raise her eyes to his. He stood and moved away as she finished picking up what remained of her things. Soon he was back and thrusting a handful of paper napkins at her.

"You'll want to wipe off all the slush before you put those things back in your pocketbook," he explained.

"It doesn't matter. I have to get back to the atelier." She shoved everyting into the handbag, knowing what he had suggested was correct, regretting that she was soiling the lining of the gray leather bag, which was newly purchased. But she was anxious to get away from him. She didn't care about the expensive bag as much as about the vivid burn of her cheeks.

"What about the money?" he asked.

"The money? What money?" Hadn't she paid for the sandwiches already? She was utterly confused. She eyed the door anxiously.

"The money on the floor," he explained.

She looked at Jacques incredulously. Here was an artist whose canvases sold for as much as $50,000 apiece and he was concerned about a few coins lost beneath the slush-covered boots of strangers.

"It doesn't matter," she repeated. It dawned on her that the publicity about Power as a slum boy who had made it on his own in the capricious and exceedingly tight art world was probably true. "I just regret losing the subway tokens. I'll have to stand in line to buy more this evening." She looked down at the floor and into her handbag. Satisfied that all her possessions were there, she clasped it shut.

"Thank you for your help. I really *do* have to be getting back to the atelier. My friend will be waiting for his lunch." She reached for the paper bag. Remembering her promise to Richard Bauman, she gave Jacques a polite, tight smile that did not engage her eyes.

He reached under the thick sheepskin jacket and thrust one hand into a pocket of his blue jeans.

"Here, take these," he offerred. In his extended palm lay two subway tokens.

She looked up at him in surprise. His unexpected gesture made her wary. Was this an offer of peace?

"No, but thank you anyway. I probably have some more in the office." She knew she had none, but she was reluctant to take even a token from Power. Before long, he would be asking her to get him a coffee in return.

"Do you want to have dinner tonight?" he asked her suddenly.

Vanessa opened her mouth in surprise. "You astonish me, Mr. Power. One minute you're calling me a spinster and the next inviting me out to dinner." She knew what he was thinking. He was certain she was an uptight, frustrated woman who just needed a man to soften her. She allowed what Maynard called "the cold look" to settle over her features. The look had always protected her from unwelcome advances and it did not fail her now. In return she saw the bored look return to cloud his eyes, the same look that she had seen on his face in Bauman's office that morning.

"I take it that means you're busy," he said without inflection.

"Yes, I have other plans. Thank you." Businesslike and firm, that's how she wanted to appear.

"Suit yourself," he replied. "Well, see you around."

He turned and left the deli by the door to the street. The encounter was over so quickly that she could but stand and stare after him, momentarily embarrassed when he turned and caught her look. He waved nonchalantly as he passed in front of the plate-glass window. She watched the back of his sheepskin jacket walking east in the direction of Park Avenue South, his loping stride carrying him away quickly. He made no effort to avoid the dirty puddles of melting snow on the sidewalk.

With a small twinge of regret she rode the slow elevator to the seventh floor where the atelier lay. She had no plans except for the Christmas shopping, which nagged at her needlessly. She was aware that plenty of time still remained before the holiday to buy the few items she needed for her small circle of family and friends. But she was a methodical, organized person: She had wanted to beat the crush of shoppers and to find a decent selection of gifts in the stores she preferred. And yet to have dinner with Jacques Power! She *had* been tempted. But at the same time she found herself highly irritated by his probing rudeness. He was a man who would say whatever crossed his mind, that was obvious. No, she knew she had made the correct decision. He was crass. He was an old-fashioned male chauvinist, a throwback to another era. A famous man on the make. Maynard had told her that Power was a womanizer and Vanessa had never had reason to doubt Maynard. She wasn't an artist's groupie; she who dealt with artists every day of her working life found them highly overrated and not one whit more fascinating than other men—just more difficult. She had sometimes secretly laughed at their well-known "sensitivity," which frequently made them more touchy to deal with than a room filled with hungry four-year-old children.

"Any messages?" she asked at the reception desk.

"Mr. Finer called. He has to cancel dinner tomorrow. Unexpected trip to Bucharest or Budapest, I forget which. He'll call you when he gets back next week." The elderly receptionist handed her a pink memo with Douglas's name on it.

"Does he want me to call back?"

"No, he won't be available. He's leaving late this afternoon.

"Thanks, Katie."

She dropped off Maynard's lunch in the temperature-controlled library room where, as a curator, he catalogued and stored all the finished prints. Maynard was nowhere to be seen, so she returned to her own office, quickly ate her cheese sandwich, and turned her attention to the French landscape that had occupied her efforts all that morning. But she could not easily forget Jacques Power and his unexpected invitation to dinner.

Chapter Two

"Will that be cash or charge, madam?" asked the mock-cultivated voice of the saleswoman behind the glove counter at Saks Fifth Avenue.

"Charge, please." Vanessa reached into her handbag for the small leather case in which she carried her driver's license and charge cards. She rummaged through the still gritty items.

"Your card?" asked the saleswoman impatiently. A line of Christmas shoppers jostled behind Vanessa.

"Just a moment. I'm looking for my charge cards. I can't seem to find them." She set the portfolio she was carrying at her feet and removed her coin purse and appointment book from her handbag, laying them on the counter before her. She shook her handbag. A taste of panic welled up in her throat. Suddenly the first floor of Saks seemed stiflingly hot, the perfume in the air cloying and oppressive. Pinpricks of perspiration burst on her skin beneath the cashmere sweater. She untied the belt of her camel coat and allowed it to fall open to admit the cool air from the street door near where she stood. "I've lost my

cards! Oh, my God, my license too! What am I going
to do?''

"Pay cash?'' suggested the salesclerk with ill-
concealed impatience.

Without a word Vanessa turned her handbag out on
the counter. A lipstick rolled away and fell at her feet.
The saleswoman was already reaffixing the price tag
on the leather gloves. She moved away silently to help
another customer. Vanessa gathered up her possessions for the second time that day and stuffed them
into the sandy handbag. She forced herself to think
clearly. The red card case must have dropped on the
floor of the deli. She hoped the staff who knew her
and knew where she worked had found it. Tomorrow
she would get the card case back. But, if not.... She
shuddered to think of the inconvenience of canceling
all her credit cards, of replacing her driver's license.
And just before Christmas. How could she even cash
a check now without those all-important documents?

Dejected, she left Saks by the Forty-ninth Street
door and crossed Fifth Avenue. It had begun to snow
again and the wind blew against her in wet gusts as she
walked west to the Sixth Avenue subway. She would
have loved to find a taxi, but she did not even raise
her head to look for one, knowing how rare an empty
cab was at five thirty, never mind the snow, which
was falling heavily now. The acrid smell of wet wool
on the train made her wish she had chosen to walk
home despite the wet streets. She was certainly in no
hurry to return to her quiet apartment. An empty evening stretched before her since, without her credit
cards and identification, she was unable to do the

Christmas shopping she had planned. She glanced down to check the portfolio at her feet. Perhaps she'd get some work done.

Leaving the mailroom of the apartment building, Vanessa was intercepted by a petite birdlike woman of advanced age, her neighbor, Miss Weissman.

"Vanessa, my dear, a quick word with you." Lena's eyes twinkled with intrigue. She had never married and her age was a closely guarded secret, but Vanessa calculated that she most probably would not see seventy again. She knew the woman meant kindness, but Lena tended to be a busybody. With little else to do, she and her lonely widowed friends, the original tenants of the West Side apartment building that had been built in the 1930's, had devoted themselves to finding Vanessa a second husband. Between them the ladies presided over a seemingly endless supply of grandsons, nephews and great-nephews, young professional men, few of whom lived in the City, but made the trip in from Long Island or New Jersey. At Maynard's urging and to be polite, she had accepted a few blind dates in the second year of her widowhood. First there had been William, the high school physical education teacher, whose idea of fun was touch football in the park on Sunday afternoons followed by one-on-one wrestling at any time. After him had come Jerry, a young public defender for the City of New York. Jerry had been more interesting perhaps because of the hilarious and sometimes heartbreaking stories he would tell her about his indigent clients, but he was two inches shorter than Vanessa, who stood five eight in her stocking feet, and he had a serious

heart condition. She had forgotten the name of the
next "eligible" bachelor presented by her kindly
neighbor, but she remembered that the man was already bald and that his mother had actually called him
at the restaurant where he had taken Vanessa to dinner. Called him twice. She had sworn that was the last
time.

"Forget the matchmaking, Lena. Your candidates
always backfire. If I'm meant to remarry, someone
will come along. And if not, my life is lovely just the
way it is, thank you."

"So you think!" Lena had answered. "One more, I
have one more. A nice boy, not a dentist, I swear.
He's nice looking, this one I've met. He travels a lot
to Europe. He comes from a nice family. Just try one
more for me. His name is Douglas Finer and I already
gave him your number."

Nice. He *was* nice. Nice man, nice-looking, nice
job, nice family. Vanessa had been going out with him
on and off for the past year. Douglas took her to good
ethnic restaurants and knew what to order. They attended concerts and gallery openings and Douglas
talked knowledgeably about composers and artists. He
was often away on business, but when he was in New
York, she saw him weekly and sometimes twice a
week. There was not a thing wrong with Douglas except that he was *nice*.

Lena leaned toward her conspiratorially. "So how's
Douglas?" she asked.

"Fine. He invited me to go home with him for the
holidays—"

"To meet his mother."

"He didn't mention his mother. I think he simply thought it would be nice for me. Of course, I had to say no. We're much too busy at work at the end of the year. No one gets time off until after New Year's, and Christmas falls in the middle of the week." Not that I would have gone, she added silently. She'd been grateful to have such a true excuse at her fingertips when Douglas had offered.

"I have it on good authority," whispered Lena, "that he is going to propose to you."

"Oh, no, Lena." Vanessa tossed her head back and laughed. "Not Douglas, not propose! Why he's barely kissed me good night in a whole year! It's not like that at all between Douglas and me, believe me."

"Mark my words, young lady. He invited you home to meet his mother. Are you certain you can't go?"

"Cannot and will not go. Douglas is just—well, he's just someone to go out with. That's all." Lena had to be wrong. She could think of few things that would surprise her more than a proposal from Douglas. There was nothing wrong with him; in fact, Lena and her two friends were on the right track. With his sandy hair and regular features, with his lucrative job at the pharmaceutical company, Douglas Finer would make some girl a perfect husband. Vanessa just wasn't that girl. The three elderly women had followed Douglas's tepid courtship avidly, perched like three goldfinches at their habitual post on the long couch in the lobby, thin legs too short to reach the marble floor. Each night Vanessa went out with Douglas, there they sat like the proverbial three monkeys. Evil they cared little for, but they saw, heard, and spoke of everything else that passed by the microcosm of the West Side lobby. How in keeping with Douglas's character to tell the old biddies before asking the prospective bride.

She let herself into the apartment, reflecting that coming home on a winter evening was no longer so bleak since she had taken to leaving a light burning in the living room. Before that, she had often felt as if she were coming into the apartment of an acquaintance whose plants she had promised to water. The apartment could still seem to be that of a stranger, but the rooms were not quite as forbidding when the lamp was glowing.

She slipped off her boots and left them on a plastic mat just within the front door. She really had overdone the redecorating, she admitted to herself. The gray industrial carpeting—that was what made it so gloomy, she decided. Yet she had invested so much money in the scheme, there seemed to be no way to rectify the mistake without being frivolous. And frivolity was one characteristic Vanessa did not have. Despite the aristocratic appearance she projected to others, she knew how practical and utilitarian she was at heart. She even wondered at times if she were dull. The redecoration, during which she had sold, given, or thrown away every piece of furniture that she and Andrew had shared, represented her psychological break with the past and its painful memories. A bit too extreme a break, which she now regretted.

She crossed the large white-walled living room in her stockings and immediately entered the kitchen to put on a kettle of water for tea. While she waited for the water to boil, she hung up her clothes and removed her makeup. She took a thick terry-cloth robe from the bedroom closet and slipped it on over her underwear. On the breast pocket of the bathrobe was a gold crest that proclaimed it had come from the Hotel George V in Paris. Maynard had given her the robe as a joke, saying he was scandalized that she chosen to stay in a small pension on the Left Bank in Paris instead of in a deluxe hotel. She had hated the pension, the trip, and yes, even Paris, but she would never had told Maynard so. At the time he had been in an unbearably affected Francophile phase, due to his then involvement with a has-been French film director. Her trip to Paris had also been an attempt to break with the past and she had learned some things about herself, mainly that she despised traveling alone.

The telephone rang twice as she poured a cup of herbal tea. When she answered, the person on the other end hung up. Vanessa was not unduly alarmed. There had been no heavy breathing and she had an unlisted number just so that no one could pick her name out of the phone book at random, figuring correctly that an initial and a last name meant a woman who lived alone.

She sat in a black leather and rosewood Eames chair, one extravagant purchase she had never regretted. She rested her stockinged feet on the matching ottoman and flipped through the mail she had picked up in the lobby, setting bills to one side and preparing to open the large, handwritten envelopes that obviously contained Christmas cards. Many postmarks indicated that they originated in her hometown of Cleveland, but she did not recognize all the married names of her school friends on the return addresses.

The doorbell rang. It had to be Lena again.

"Be right there," she called, putting her teacup down with a sigh. She opened the door without a thought, knowing that anyone from outside the building would have to ring up from the lobby.

Jacques Power filled the doorway, his thatch of red hair plastered to his well-shaped head by the wet snow. In one arm he held a grease-stained brown bag.

"Do you always open the door without asking who's there?" he opened without preliminary.

"How did you get by the doorman?" she asked in genuine surprise. "What are you doing here, anyway?"

"I knew you had lied to me about being busy tonight, so I came over," he answered maddeningly.

"I did *not* lie. I was busy." Irritation and embarrassment at being caught in a bathrobe and without shoes or makeup overwhelmed her.

"If you're busy, why are you home? You look like you're in for the night," he answered with infuriating logic.

"Because my plans changed. What do *you* want here?" She hadn't meant to speak so abruptly, but she made no effort to soften the question. What *was* he doing at her apartment door?

"I brought dinner. May I come in?" he said. But he had already pushed past her and stood in the foyer even as he asked the question.

"I believe you already *are* in. What do you mean

you brought dinner? You didn't even know I'd be at home. How did you know where I live? You're dripping on the rug."

"Sorry about that. I'll take off my boots."

"I didn't say you could stay."

"Well, kick me out, then. But you'll miss the best Chinese food on the West Side." He held up the grease-stained paper bag as if to prove what he said was true.

She smelled the exotic odors that wafted from the unpromising-looking bag and realized she was hungry. Mentally she inventoried the contents of the refrigerator. All she could remember was a container of peach yogurt of uncertain age and two frozen diet dinners.

"What the hell, come in. But leave your boots on the mat."

"Yes, ma'am." Jacques set the bag down and removed his water-spotted sheepskin jacket. She took it from him to hang in the hall closet. It smelled of fresh air and the cold. And the evocative scent of male and leather.

Jacques unlaced his boots and pulled them off. His big toe stuck through a two-inch hole in his wool socks.

"I think you need a new pair of socks. You'll get blisters," she said, immediately sorry she had made such a motherly comment.

"I can't be bothered with details like that," he answered airily, rankling her with his offhanded attitude. He walked ahead of her into the living room. "Where shall I put the food?"

"In the kitchen. Around to the right. I'll just put on some clothes—"

"Don't bother, you look fine. I like to see a woman wearing a man's clothes."

"I'm not wearing a man's clothes. This is *my* bathrobe." She looked down at her unshod feet. The voluminous bathrobe covered her modestly, yet under his probing eyes, she felt naked beneath the thick folds of terry cloth. "No, I'll change. I'll just be a moment." As he followed her directions to the kitchen, she entered the bedroom and firmly closed the door behind her. She slipped off the snowy robe and stood in front of the open double doors of the closet in a blue lace slip, undecided about what to wear. His sudden arrival, his presence in her kitchen, had made her head whirl. She heard him shout through the door.

"This isn't at all what I expected your place to look like."

"What did you expect—stuffed animals on the bed?" she shouted back.

"I haven't seen the bed yet," he answered from directly behind her. "Perhaps you'll show it to me."

She turned in a panic to see his tall frame in the doorway. She made a lunge for the robe, which lay on the bed, and held it protectively before her. "Get out of here! You're certainly sure of yourself. I barely know you. I can assure you that a couple of tokens and a Chinese dinner aren't going to get you in bed with *me*! Maybe your groupies throw themselves at your feet—"

"Hey, slow down. It was only a little joke, but I can see you have no sense of humor," he said smoothly.

He held long-fingered hands in front of himself, palms out, in a gesture of defense. A sardonic little grin played across his features.

"I have a great sense of humor," she said defensively. "I just don't think you're funny. Merely irritating." She was blushing furiously, to her unbridled annoyance.

"Touché. I put the food in the kitchen. I'll wait out here for you." He gave her a long look she could not interpret and closed the door softly behind him when he went out.

"Some nerve," she muttered under her breath. She threw on a floor-length paisley caftan that totally covered the lines of her willowy body. As she dressed she wondered if he would still be there when she came out of the bedroom. Perhaps she had been too sharp. But he had asked for it, she told herself. He was always asking for it. She had never met such a rude and abrasive man. She checked her image in the mirror on the closet door. When she was satisfied that the telltale blush had disappeared from her angular cheekbones, she opened the door quietly. She could hear him in the kitchen. She ran back to the dresser and dabbed a light floral scent behind her ears.

The tiny kitchen seemed even smaller with him in it. His dominating presence filled the narrow room.

"Got any wine?" he asked without looking up from the white cartons of food he took from the paper bag. He made no reference to the scene in the bedroom.

"Not to go with Chinese food, I don't think." She decided not to mention the bedroom either.

"I'm not fussy. And I didn't expect the Four Seasons. I'll drink what you have."

Vanessa had to squeeze past him to reach the refrigerator. She sucked in her stomach so as not to touch him. But as she brushed past his body she felt the hard muscles of his arm and she smelled the same tangy scent she had noticed on his sheepskin jacket. *Be careful,* she admonished herself. She would have to control herself and the situation.

"Just some white wine. Is this all right?" She held up an almost-full bottle of undistinguished California wine.

"Fine, fine. I'll just look around while you set things up."

He might set things up while I *look around. This dinner is his idea, after all,* she thought to herself. But she meekly assented to gather plates, wineglasses, and silverware. Acquiescing was preferable to his nosing around the cabinets and drawers of her kitchen. She had a notion that he would be unable to wash a glass. Or that he even cared about having a clean glass at all.

"You have a fantastic collection of prints here," he called from the living room. "But your place is not at all what I expected."

"You said that before. What do you mean?"

"It's kind of sterile."

"What had you expected?"

"Oh, more clutter, I suppose. Traditional furniture. Chintz...pillows...a cat. You're the preppy type, the kind who does needlepoint on everything. Your apartment doesn't look like you."

She stopped and stared at him as she came out of

the kitchen. He had nearly described what her apartment had looked like before. Yellow floral chintz. Cherry furniture. But no cat. Andrew had been allergic to cats, although Vanessa loved them.

"I thought this building was co-op," he commented, turning from where he had been admiring the framed prints on the wall. He caught her wondering stare.

"It is," she answered. She forced her eyes to look away. She set the tray down on the plate glass and bronze coffee table. He must have spent time thinking about her to have so accurately assessed her personality. She surreptitiously glanced around the room to see if she had left her needlepoint project out. For some reason she did not want Jacques to know how unerring his incisive observations had been. He made her wary and uncomfortable, even a bit fearful, although she could not imagine why she should react to him with fear. She poured two glasses of wine. "Cheers," she toasted him flatly, holding up her glass.

"Cheers," he echoed and drained the glass.

Vanessa sipped her wine slowly. She had no intention of letting herself get drunk and careless around Jacques Power.

"How do you know so much about the West Side? What buildings are co-op, the best Chinese food? Do you live around here?"

"No. My studio is in SoHo," he said.

"Of course, the 'in' place. I should have known."

"Yeah, but I've been down there for fifteen years and it wasn't 'in' then. Used to have to go to New

Jersey to buy my groceries. Now it's all gussied up—
boutiques, galleries, cute restaurants. I'm thinking of
moving. Can't stand all that pseudo-artsy stuff.''

"Moving? Where to?" A crazy thought that she
did not want him to move crossed her mind.

"Oh, I don't know. I could work anywhere, I suppose. I don't need to be around the market anymore
like I used to. Now they come to me. They'd still
come whether I lived in Chattanooga or Odessa, that's
for sure.''

"Absolutely. You certainly know what you're
worth," she observed dryly.

"That's not conceit, honey. Just reality.''

"My name is Vanessa, not 'honey.'"

"Better than Miss VanderPoel anyway." They sipped their wine in silence.

"Shall I serve the food?" she asked.

"Go ahead." He stood and circled the large living
room, stopping to examine the prints hanging gallery
style on the stark, white walls. "Where did you get
this fabulous collection?" he asked her.

"Of prints or frames? Collecting antique frames is
my hobby. I get them all around—junk stores, antique
shops, garage sales in the country." Without realizing
how she had warmed to the subject, she talked on. It
pleased her that he was both interested and confused
by her apartment. "As for the prints, they're one of
the fringe benefits of my job. Those are all lithographs
that I separated. The artist—" She hesitated, embarrassed to be explaining something he should have
known.

"Go on," he encouraged.

"The artists usually give me a dedicated print when we've finished the job."

"There must be forty of them here. Is that why you've done up your place like a gallery?"

"Well, partly, I suppose. When the building went co-op, I had some renovations done and it seemed logical to redecorate at the time. A change, you know. A change is sometimes good. . . ." Her voice trailed off.

"So you do own this place! You're rich. I knew it the first time I saw you. And that name—VanderPoel. Very elegant. I suppose you went to private schools."

She saw no reason to point out that her name was not VanderPoel, except by marriage. What difference did her name make, anyway? And an inbred sense of privacy made her reluctant to explain that without the money from Andrew's life insurance policy, she would never have been able to buy this apartment when the building went co-operative.

"I am not rich, not at all. Yes, I attended a private school, but so do lots of people. She had been about to say "just like you," but the red-haired artist was no ordinary person. At least he was unlike any ordinary person Vanessa had met. Power obviously had some hang-up about his background. Why else would he resent the implication of privilege in hers? "But my financial matters are of no concern of yours, are they?" she said pointedly. She had thought Jacques and she could have a friendly conversation, but now she saw she'd been wrong. He was incredibly nosy. She was unused to dealing with such directness.

They ate in silence. It was Jacques who finally spoke.

"I often say the wrong thing. It's part of my character."

"Not an endearing aspect of your personality," she observed between bites of something dark brown and fiery hot. "But I suppose you can get away with it. After all, you're a celebrity." What made him so irritating? His self-assurance? His insolence? She knew he would make a pass at her, that he would expect her to fall into bed with him as a matter of course. She had spent the past eight years dealing with famous and temperamental artists who printed their lithographs at Columbia Atelier. She had learned to read them well. They expected to be treated differently from other people. She supposed it was all the publicity they read about themselves in the press. Her private theory was that fame corrupted their power of judgment. This one would be surprised, however. She was not impressed by his fame. Nor by his looks, she told herself. Although his disheveled red hair had begun to appeal to her slightly. And the freckles that covered his nose and cheeks. Such an incongruous appearance for a famous painter! She was unaware that she was regarding him intently, one well-shaped eyebrow quirked as she appraised his unusual looks.

"What are you staring at?" he asked her suddenly.

"Staring? Was I? I'm sorry." She cleared her throat nervously.

"What's so interesting?" he persisted.

"I didn't realize I was, but if you insist, I was thinking how unlike a celebrity you do look."

"I'm just me. I didn't ask to be a big celebrity, you know. It just happened."

"But now that you are one, you like it," she pursued.

"Not much. Not much at all."

"Not even the advantages—the privilege of being known, of getting what you want just because you are who you are?"

"You mean like getting the best tables, not having to wait in line? Things like that?" He was teasing her, she could see the laughing look around his eyes once again.

"No, I wasn't thinking of things like that."

"What were you thinking of? Women?"

"Um...yes."

"They are part of what I *don't* like. The women."

"I'm sure," she said, her voice heavy with sarcasm. "I'm not your type," she hastened to add.

"Who said you were? Who asked?"

"I—I just wanted to get that clear from the start," she said quickly, flustered that the conversation had taken such a turn and acutely aware, to her own surprise, that she herself had made it happen.

"You're scared to death of me. I'm not going to rape you, young lady. Is your innocence so precious? Innocence in a woman your age puts you into the category of an antique, you know." His eyes crinkled with laughter and deep dimples appeared at either side of his wide mouth.

Vanessa jumped off the sofa as if stung by a bee. She began to gather up the half-full containers of Chinese food, the paper napkins. She made herself busy so she would not look into the jaded green eyes she felt on her. She threw a soiled fork on the tray.

"Disappointed?" he asked.

"Not at all. I don't believe in mixing business with pleasure." The muscles in her jaws worked. She did not want him to see how angry she felt. She usually thought of herself as a calm person, one who was slow to boil. But Jacques Power made her see red with disturbing frequency. From the moment they met in Bauman's office, he had knocked her off balance. She did not want him to see the power he exercised over her emotions. She kept her head down as she picked up the remains of the Chinese dinner, hoping he did not notice the telltale patches of red she was certain stained her cheeks. With an effort she suppressed her anger and said as smoothly as she could manage, "You had better go now. I have work—"

The telephone rang. Gratefully she turned her back on Jacques, hiding her face from his sardonic eyes.

Without preamble Maynard's smooth voice came through the wire. "There's the most fabulous Claudette Colbert film on Channel—"

"I can't talk now, Maynard. I have a visitor," she interrupted.

"Anyone I know?" he asked knowingly. Although her back was to him, she was aware of Jacques's warmth a few feet away. She knew he could probably hear Maynard's voice from where he sat, although she doubted he could make out the words of their conversation.

"Know *of*, professionally speaking," she answered. Maynard was so attuned to her, she was certain he would guess almost immediately who was in the apartment with her.

"Has to do with the atelier?"

"Quite recently, as a matter of fact," she answered glibly.

"A sexy redhead!" he announced.

"Smart boy," she affirmed.

"Well, my dear, I won't intrude. No doubt you have matters pending. Forget Claudette Colbert. See you tomorrow and you can tell me all."

"As little as it will be," she rejoined with assurance.

"One last thing, Vanessa. 'The great artists of the world are never Puritans, and seldom even ordinarily respectable.' See you tomorrow." He hung up before she could ask him whom he was quoting.

She returned to the coffee table and bent to pick up Jacques's empty plate. He reached out and closed his long-fingered hand over her wrist.

"Who was that, the man with the bathrobe?"

"As a matter of fact, yes, that's exactly who it was," she replied, staring down as if hypnotized by the freckled hand that held her arm captive. Her skin burned at his touch and a languid warmth diffused throughout her body. What was happening to her resolve? She raised her eyebrows and looked questioningly into his eyes. "Although the bathrobe does belong to me. A souvenir of a trip to Paris." Let him think she and Maynard had made the trip together. Jacques would probably never have occasion to meet Maynard at the atelier. And even if the two men met, she doubted that Jacques would be able to realize from Maynard's good looks and debonair manner what was obvious to those who knew the curator well.

Why should she bother to explain Maynard's lack of sexual interest in her or any other woman? Power had no right to question her about telephone calls anyway. She attempted to keep her voice calm, to not betray by even the flicker of an eyelash that she found his grip on her wrist the slightest bit out of the ordinary. The touch of his warm skin on hers dizzied her. When she finally spoke, her voice quivered. The words sounded to her as if she were speaking from underwater.

"I think you had better go now."

In answer he reached out and removed the empty plate from her other hand, setting it down abruptly on the table. The china clattered on the beveled glass. He grasped her by the now free hand and pulled her down next to him on the sofa, making the leather sigh when she sank into its yielding depths. He was so near she felt pulsing vibrations running between their bodies, as if an electric current crackled between them. He leaned his face closer to hers, forcing her against the back of the sofa. His hands still held both her wrists in a firm, but painless grasp. She inhaled unevenly.

"You had better go," she repeated slowly, finding difficulty forming the nearly inaudible words.

"You don't want me to go," he answered quietly. He now held her hands tightly, capturing her gaze as well with the hypnotic intensity of his gold-flecked hazel eyes. She knew he heard the beating of her heart although she barely heard anything through the pounding of the blood rushing in her ears. His thumb rubbed a gentle, tight circle on her inner wrist. She tingled under his touch.

"What is that perfume you wear? You smell like the first flowers of spring."

"It's...uh...it's lily of the valley." His eyes were ever closer. She could barely tolerate looking into their green depths. The warmth within her grew and pulsated. She tried to close her own eyes, but she was unable to break the spell of his look. His face closed in on hers, blurring slowly. When she did not resist the warm lips that brushed hers lightly, he pressed against her mouth with a shockingly sudden urgency. She tried to pull her head back, but she was trapped between Jacques's mouth and the back of the sofa. Almost against her will, her lips parted beneath his insistent mouth and her insides seemed to melt. He dropped her hands and wrapped his arms roughly around her waist, pulling her yielding body to his hard and muscular torso. She was lost in the demand of him, her body pressing against his with the same fiery urgency his mouth telegraphed. Her steely resolve began to trickle away. She twined her fingers in his curly red hair and pulled his head closer to her own. He lowered his lips to her neck and buried his face there.

She was willing to yield when he pushed her down beneath him on the butter-soft leather of the couch. He ran one hand up her leg, under the caftan, under the lace slip, trailing his fingers along the nylon that covered her thigh. She trembled and he shifted his body to cover hers, anchoring her more firmly beneath him. Before she could remind herself that she was afraid of him, his mouth seized hers again, tearing through her thoroughly demoralized defenses

with an ease she would not have thought possible five
minutes before. Her lips parted willingly now, and she
put her tongue into his mouth, recognizing the sweet
scent of desire on his breath. Dreamily she imagined
he tasted the same want in her. His hard body pressed
against her. She shivered again at the knowing stroke
of his hand on her leg, responding to his caresses by
wrapping her arms tightly around his muscular back,
knowing from the feel of him against her that he was
as aroused as she.

In a gesture of impatience he roughly pushed the
caftan and slip up around her waist, exposing her legs
and the smooth skin of her stomach. He kissed the
bared skin, burying his mouth and nose against her.
Shocks of pleasure shot through her. Subtle, rippling
thrills seemed to leave his mouth and enter her body,
radiating outward to warm every finger and toe.

At first she hardly heard his mumbled words. A
moment passed before their meaning sunk in to her
fevered brain.

"So, you *are* alive, after all. I thought there might
be something under that icy exterior."

Vanessa sat erect and put her hands on his chest,
shoving him away with all the strength she could
muster. The wrench between her anger at his insolence and a mounting desire for him made her head
spin with frustration. She pulled the caftan quickly
over her bare legs.

"Why don't you just leave? If you want someone
easy, you must know hundreds of women who are
willing. Why do you want to complicate *my* life?" She
jumped up from the couch, adjusting the caftan, and

paced the room. "What are you doing here, anyway? How did you find me?"

"What's the big deal? You want me—that's obvious. And I want you. That must be equally obvious. So, why not? Sex doesn't have to 'complicate' your life, as you put it. Let's just enjoy each other."

"I'm not a fan of casual sex, that's why. I—I believe in commitment. You think *everybody* wants you. What an ego!" she sputtered. *And I'm one of that crowd,* she admitted silently, shocked to recognize the physical need for him that shook her to the core.

"And you expect me to believe that you don't feel desire for me? What was that a minute ago, an imitation of passion? Come on, get off your soapbox."

"Well," she answered feebly, "we *do* have to work together. It isn't good business." The argument sounded weak, even to her own ears, but in her heart she knew she was correct. She feared Jacques and an involvement with him. Perhaps it was Maynard's warnings working on her subconscious. She checked an impulse to walk across the room to him, to put her arm on his, to ask him to try to understand how *she* felt. She shook off the impulse. He was an artist, after all. It was too much to ask him to accept a middle-class value such as commitment. Love 'em and leave 'em—that was more his style.

"We're *not* going to be working together, I told you that already. I do my own work and that's that. I don't need you. Or anybody, for that matter. I got where I am because of me—no one else. So that argument doesn't hold water. You're really a high-strung person. Why not just let down your hair and have a good

time? Nothing ventured, nothing gained, you know.
If you don't take a risk, you'll never know ecstasy.
That's what life's all about, Vanessa.''

"That's the fail-proof line, right? Well, thank you
for the philosophy lesson, Jacques. I know about taking risks and frankly, I don't care to."

"What are you afraid of?"

She did not answer him immediately. She picked at
an invisible spot on the paisley caftan. What *was* she
afraid of? Being a scalp on his belt of conquests? Being laughed at by the mocking hazel eyes that now
regarded her so intently? Falling in love with him?
She could never fall in love with such a rude, egotistical boor. Andrew had been the epitome of sensitivity,
of cultivated gentility. Andrew was the type of man
who had always attracted her, not the aggressive redhead who still lounged casually on the leather couch
across the room. He would never understand the scars
that held her back from him—or from any other man
she could not be certain of. Jacques had just told her
in exact words that he stood alone in his world, that
he eschewed the help of any person. Vanessa did not
want another emotionally independent man in her
life; marriage to Andrew had broken her spirit. And
here was Jacques mouthing almost the same words
she had heard from Andrew a score of times. "I don't
need your help." "No one can help me, I have to
work this out myself." And, near the end, "Leave me
alone—I don't want to see you. I need to get away by
myself." On just such a flight from her, he had
crashed the car into a bridge abutment on the Long
Island Expressway. An accident, the policeman who

came to the door that winter afternoon had said, as gently as he could. "Your husband's had an accident." But Vanessa knew it had been no accident, although no one had questioned her and so she had shared her dark knowledge with no one.

She searched for a valid-sounding answer to his question. Unbidden, the placid face of Douglas Finer flitted across her thoughts. Good old Douglas, a handy excuse.

"Look, Jacques. I'm already committed to someone," she lied. "It's not fair to lead you on. I'm in no position to get involved with you no matter how casually. Why did you come here tonight, anyway?"

Jacques stood and stretched. "Where's my jacket?" He walked easily to the front hall of the apartment. As he bent to pull on his boots, she looked down on his wild red hair and thought incongruously how easily he gave up. Yet hadn't she wanted him to stop? But now, knowing he was about to leave, she was no longer certain. Oh, how he confused her! The jumbled emotions he stirred in her gave her no peace.

"I came by because I thought I'd been a bit pushy with you this morning. I knew where you lived because I picked up your identification cards in the deli this afternoon. I didn't realize I still had them until I was back at the loft." He handed her the small red case that contained her official life.

"Thank you for the dinner, it was delicious. I hope you have no hard feelings." She wanted to ask him to stay. She wanted him to put his long arms around her and to hold on tightly until morning, perhaps to never let go, but she was unable to say the words that would detain him. A knot of fear closed her throat. He was gazing at her again with those deep hazel eyes, but no laughlines played around the edges now. She leaned to him slightly, certain he was about to kiss her, yet he made no move toward her. He buttoned the honey-colored sheepskin jacket.

"If you change your mind, give me a call. *I'm* available," he said lightly. His hand fumbled with the doorknob. "How do you get out of here, anyway?"

Vanessa reached in front of him and undid the upper lock. Once more her hand brushed across his. She heard her own sharp intake of breath. Suddenly one long arm closed around her neck and pulled her mouth to his. They exchanged a long and hungry kiss. Once more she smelled the heady aroma of man and leather. She stepped back and inhaled deeply, wanting more of his evocative scent in her nostrils, anxious for him to leave, longing for him to stay. She was unsettled, unable to choose what she really desired to happen. But before she could decide, the door was open and Jacques was halfway down the hall. By the time she realized that she was no longer in his arms he was at the elevator, punching the call button fiercely. But he turned to her steadily and gave a mock salute, the same cynical little smile already playing on his wide lips. Wordlessly she stepped back and closed the apartment door. Her legs were trembling and her knees threatened to buckle beneath her. She leaned her forehead against the cool painted metal, unable to gather her wits or to understand what had just transpired between them.

Chapter Three

She saw Jacques at the atelier frequently during the following week. Saw him, but did not speak with him. He never sought her out to talk to her. For her own part, she had been so unsettled by the earth-shaking physical attraction for him she had discovered within herself, touched off by his unexpected visit to her apartment, that she did not dare approach him. She wavered between a need to draw close to him, to touch his warm skin, and a burning desire to tell him off, to shout to him that she was not like other women he was obviously accustomed to seeing—and bedding.

When the machines began to run his first lithograph she watched him covertly through the glass wall of her office as he stood next to the master printer, checking the first proofs to roll off the thundering press, adjusting each new color as it was overlayed. He pointedly ignored her, although by now he was certainly aware that her office was located right off the printing room. She used every opportunity to study him, to notice the way his wiry red hair curled over the back of his shirt collar. Noted that he needed a haircut, that a small hole was widening on the knee of his blue jeans. Was aware of the day he wore a stiff, new pair of denim pants, but that the jeans were already blotched with paint, as if he painted in the early morning, before coming to the atelier. She wondered about his studio, what he ate for breakfast, where he went when the workday was over—and with whom.

She could play his game too, she vowed. Those times she sensed that he was watching her—she felt his hazel eyes on her as if they were his very hands—she refused to heed his glances. Publicly it was as if they had never met, had never shared those few moments of kindled desire for one another.

She knew from Maynard that Jacques was having trouble separating the colors of his vibrant lithographs, but she also knew that he would never ask for *her* help. With time and experimentation he would get the hues right. He would find it extremely laborious; she could have done all the prints in his series in the time he probably needed to complete just one. But that was his problem, she told herself each time she noticed a look of angry frustration on his freckled face as a new proof rolled off the press. Bauman had not come to her for anything, so whatever Jacques had told her employer about working alone must have sunk in.

Maynard teased her, accused her of mooning distractedly in the office. More than once he had seen her staring at Jacques and lost in thought.

"'Love's a disease. But curable,'" he quoted, popping his head into her office door one afternoon. Her mouth fell open in surprise, but before she could reply, he was gone.

She was ready the next time he stuck his head around the doorframe and said, "'How alike are the groans of love to those of the dying.'"

"Stop, Maynard. Who said that?" she asked quickly.

"Malcolm Lowry. Do you know his works?"

"No. And I'm not in love. Why are you teasing me like this?"

"Well, my dear, you aren't yourself. I warned you about Power, you know."

"There's nothing to warn me about, Maynard. I told you nothing happened that night," she said. She regretted having told him anything, but it was unavoidable since he *had* called while Jacques was at her apartment.

"I know what you told me, but you haven't been the same since. What's going to happen when you see him at the Christmas party, may I ask?"

"The Christmas party! Is *he* going to be there?" she said quickly, giving herself away.

"Not that you are interested, I understand, but I did overhear Bauman invite him and his father and they accepted."

"I didn't know he had a father." She had never considered Jacques's background except for the few details she had heard about his origins on the Boston docks. Little remained of a regional accent in his speech.

"Ah, perhaps you thought he sprang fully grown

from the sea, like a masculine Venus, with a paint-brush held defiantly where a fig leaf would be."

"Maynard!" She blushed. "What is his father like?" she asked, picturing an older and slightly less abrasive version of Jacques.

"Not a gentleman." This was one of Maynard's most damning criticisms.

"What happened?"

"He came to the atelier the other day looking for Power. Apparently he needed some money. Jacques said he didn't have very much on him, would give him a check when he got home. But his dear father pulled one of Jacques's own checks out of his wallet and had him sign it right then and there. Pretty crass. Awkward for everyone in the room. Of course Bauman was fawning all over the two of them and asked the old man to the Christmas party. Jacques didn't look too enthusiastic, but his father jumped at the invitation. After the free drinks and food, I should imagine."

"How sad" was all she said.

"What are you planning to wear?" Maynard was vitally interested in clothes.

"I hadn't thought about it. My long tartan skirt and a silk blouse? It *is* Christmas."

"But, my dear, so suburban. Wear the gray silk dress, the one I made you buy at Bendel's. That's much more elegant. And pearls. I suppose Bauman's wife will be there. Oh, how dreary."

"Of course, she will. It's their apartment, after all. Poor Richard."

"I'm bringing a new friend I want you to meet. The

most inspired decorator! He's just back from doing a clutch of condominiums at Las Hadas on the west coast of Mexico. You'll love him," said Maynard, with an enthusiasm in his voice that she had not heard since his early days with the French director. "Douglas won't care for him, however."

"Douglas? Douglas isn't coming to the party. He's going home to his mother for the holidays." Douglas and Maynard didn't mix well. She would not have invited the staid Douglas to the company Christmas party in any event. Since Maynard planned to bring his new friend, she would have to attend the party alone. Well, so be it. She probably saw too much of Maynard, anyway. But without Maynard, her life would have been extremely lonely. He was a true and faithful friend.

On Saturday she set off to finish her Christmas shopping. She was at the door of Saks when the store opened. Consulting a written list, racing through various departments, anxiously one step ahead of the burgeoning holiday crowds, she bought the leather gloves for Miss Weissman, a cashmere vest for her father in Cleveland, and a ruffled camisole and matching petticoat for her niece on Andrew's side of the family. She had the packages gift-wrapped and took the gloves with her, asking that the other presents be sent by the store. The next stop on her itinerary was a tiny shop on Madison Avenue that specialized in French and English china. She had decided to add a miniature enameled box to Maynard's collection of delicate porcelains. She found exactly what she sought, an oval cream-white porcelain box, bound in brass, and overlaid with a carpet of impossibly tiny violets. It nestled in a velvet-lined fitted leather box. The inscription read, "We are all born mad. Some remain so." She bought the box, although the clerk could not tell her the source of the quotation. Maynard would know, or he would find out.

She was hungry. She bought a *Times* and found a seat at the counter of a small luncheonette. She ordered a sandwich and turned the newspaper to the Saturday art page. There, in large black letters, Jacques's name jumped out at her. A show of his works was on in a gallery only two blocks uptown from where she sat. She gulped her coffee, paid, and walked uptown, half the sandwich left on the plate. Of course, Jacques would not be there. It wasn't an opening, after all. She had never seen his work in the flesh, so to speak, only in reproduction.

A discreet buzzer sounded in the back of the gallery as she pushed open the door. The quiet was a shock after the blaring horns of Madison Avenue. A woman of indeterminate age, dressed totally in black, approached her.

"Is there anything we can help you with?" She eyed Vanessa's Saturday attire of blue jeans and boots under a violet down coat. She sniffed.

"I'd like to see the Power exhibit."

"The entire gallery is devoted to Mr. Powers's work until the end of the year." Vanessa noticed she had mispronounced Jacques's name.

"I'll just look around, then."

"Let us know if you need any assistance," the

woman answered doubtfully. She returned to the rear
of the gallery and resumed a telephone conversation.

Vanessa slowly circled the square room, stopping
before each massive canvas to study its violet splashes
of primary color. She recognized several from proofs
she had seen at the atelier, and she decided that Bauman's idea of marketing lithographs was wrong. A
small copy of the six-foot-square canvases could
never capture the power and strength of the works
before her. One oil in particular caught her attention,
a work more subdued and certainly sadder than all the
rest. A heavy build-up of pigment caught the glint of
sunlight and yet she felt the wild intensity of a raging
storm. Its main colors were slate blues and browns
and a myriad grays. Of all Jacques's paintings, the
dark one appealed to her the most. She approached
the rear of the gallery. The woman, who made Vanessa think of an undertaker, had finished her telephone conversation. She looked up reluctantly, using
a finger to mark her place in a novel she was reading.

"Number seven. Could you tell me the name of the
work? And how much it is?"

"Mr. Powers's works start at forty-eight thousand
dollars." She made no move to look up the name of
the painting.

"Perhaps they do," said Vanessa sweetly, "but that
isn't what I asked you. I would like to know the name
of the painting and its price. By the way, his name is
Power."

"I beg your pardon?"

"Power. There is no 's' in Power."

Vanessa idly picked up a printed biographical sheet

about Jacques as the saleswoman wordlessly crossed to a desk and brought back a leather-bound notebook. The woman riffled through the pages of the book until she came to one with Jacques's name written across the top in Italianate calligraphy. There followed a list of his paintings and their prices. Vanessa hardly heard the woman tell her that the painting was titled "Hudson River" and its price was $57,000. She was too busy memorizing the address of Jacques's studio, which she was able to read upside down in the notebook.

"Thank you very much!" Vanessa left the gallery quickly, oblivious of the look of surprise the clerk shot after her.

She took a downtown bus and planned to get off two or three blocks south of Jacques's address. That way, she could pick out the building safely from the privacy of the bus while she watched for him on the SoHo street. She did not ask herself what she expected to happen. She had given in long ago to the knowledge that she was obsessed with Jacques Power. Maynard had been correct in his appraisal of her state. She would not have used the word *love*: How could she be in love? She barely knew Jacques. But yes, she *was* entranced. Perhaps *infatuated* was more the word. But wary, definitely wary. She would never admit to Maynard that she no longer took a shower each night, that she soaked in the tub instead, afraid she might not hear the telephone if Jacques decided to call her.

She read the biography. He was forty, unmarried, a native of Boston. Had taken up art against the wishes of his family and worked on the docks as a stevedore to put himself through art school. After college he'd gone on to study figure drawing in London, oil painting in Paris. Had come to New York directly from Europe. He owned another home in Connecticut, but did most of his painting in the SoHo loft. She learned little from the glossy printed page.

The bus passed slowly through his block. She scanned the street in vain for his wild, red hair. She picked out his loft building, an undistinguished facade in a street of similar edifices. She disembarked from the bus at the next stop and walked uptown, preparing a little story in her head on the off-chance that she would see him on the street. She might be searching for picture frames—there had to be a junk shop somewhere in the area. She scrawled the name and address of a fictitious store on a blank page of the memo pad she carried so that she could refer to her note if he asked her what she was doing on his block. She strolled slowly up the street, her stomach churning with apprehension, her hands clammy inside the fur-lined gloves she wore. The street seemed strangely empty as she approached his building. Only one other person was visible on the block—an older woman, trying vainly to subtract twenty years from her age by means of strident hair peroxide. Hadn't the poor soul ever heard of toner? Her hair was so bleached it shone surreally green alongside the two garish splotches of crimson rouge that stained her cheeks. Her coat was unfashionably short and made Vanessa wonder idly how she could stand the cold on the red and dimpled knees that poked above white boots.

Vanessa walked uneventfully past Jacques's building seeing nothing—no one—of interest. She continued uptown for three blocks, her every sense acutely attuned to the surroundings. Jacques walked on this cement; he smelled the odors of this street, perhaps bought his groceries in the small market on the corner. The dark pub in the next block might be his favorite hangout after a long day of painting. She crossed at an intersection and turned back downtown, ambling slowly. Her toes and cheeks burned with cold. A few lonely snowflakes began to fall.

She had to pass close to the flashy blond who leaned against the building directly across from Jacques's loft. Her nose glowed red with cold. Vanessa caught a whiff of her heavy perfume. Her mind formed an image of a fluted blue bottle she had smelled in the dime store when she was a teen-ager. Something in Paris? She wrinkled her nose in distaste. Her toes were numb. Suddenly she asked herself what she was doing there. She must be out of her mind! A fool! Acting like a moon-struck teen-ager herself, walking up and down his street, hoping for a fleeting glimpse of his freckled face. She picked up speed, retracing her steps to the bus stop, eager now to be away from his neighborhood. Fearful now that she *would* meet Jacques.

She returned to her quiet apartment, embarrassed about what she had done that afternoon. Thank God he hadn't seen her. What had happened to her good judgment? She couldn't get Jacques out of her mind. But she *must* stop thinking about him. She must forget the night he had so unexpectedly come to her apartment. Must stop replaying the passionate kisses that had rekindled a fire she had thought long dead in her heart. The rude and egotistical artist was not the type of man she wanted in her life, complicating her emotions, demanding her involvement, and offering her nothing in return. She had no romantic illusions; she knew what he wanted from her. He had made his philosophy quite clear that night. That's how modern people came together now, she reflected, knowing that she was hopelessly old-fashioned. An affair with him would be short-lived at best, a one-night stand at worst. She was no one-night stand—never had been, never would be. She valued herself too highly to engage in such a tawdry solution to a perfectly natural sexual tension that grew from her attraction to an admittedly seductive man. If those were his terms, she could live without him, without any man, if need be. She had no overwhelming need for a man like Jacques Power.

Jacques found himself trapped with his back to the French doors that led to a terrace overlooking Fifth Avenue and Central Park. Mild annoyance and boredom glazed his green eyes. From time to time his tousled red head nodded in unhearing agreement with the fatuous words of the Scarsdale matron who pinned him to the leaded double doors, capturing him against his will while she regurgitated some nonsense she had picked up at a Larchmont Woman's Club lecture on the role of abstract art in the political reshaping of the Western World. The Baumans' spacious and glittering penthouse apartment vibrated with the elevated voices of ninety people enjoying the lavish ostentation of Mrs. Bauman's finely tuned social climbing. No one could convince Jacques that this was the employees' Christmas party. Sure, that's what Bauman had called it when he extended the invitation at the atelier. And sure, the printers were there, accompanied by curvaceous wives with skirts too short and hair too long. But Jacques had attended too many gatherings where he was hung up as the centerpiece, the plum, the glittering jewel in the hostess' crown of transient social achievement, not to recognize all the earmarks of a Power-on-Display occasion. He hated parties in general and this kind of pretentious party in particular.

His eyes stared past the lacquered hair of his captor and swept the room in search of rescue. He had naturally assumed that the party would take place at the atelier. That the printers and their wives would attend, drink too much, pinch the wrong behinds or kiss the wrong lips. Go home and fight over their wine-fueled indiscretions and then make up in the time-honored way. He wouldn't have minded that kind of party too much and he hadn't really objected when the old man had jumped at Bauman's invitation. But when Bauman had mentioned that they would be meeting at his Fifth Avenue penthouse, that a few friends would fill out the guest list, well, Jacques had known immediately what the evening would be like.

His eyes came to rest on Mrs. Bauman, not too difficult considering the jewelry she sported. Even from the opposite side of the crowded room, a chunky diamond glittered on her left hand and a walnut-size topaz on her right. Two diamond rocks shone from her ears, as well. A bit heavy-handed in front of the employees, he thought. He knew her type—too thin, too tan. Before she had even said hello, he'd already known that her voice would be too loud. He felt sorry for Bauman. The rumors that he had major money troubles were probably true. Even if he had not seen the luxury of their penthouse apartment, the inappropriate spread of caviar and smoked salmon and truffle-studded pâté, Jacques had already guessed at how important his contract must be to Bauman from all the bowing and scraping he'd been doing to him at the atelier. No one these days could afford a woman like Celia Bauman, not unless he had endless coffers of oil money. And he doubted that Bauman qualified on that score.

He sipped his champagne and ached for a beer. Didn't she know anything? he wondered. This was a beer and rye crowd, the employees anyway. If she had to be snobbish, she could have laid in a few cases of English ale or fine German lager. He watched Celia chat up his father as if she had captured the attention of the Prince of Wales. It was only a matter of time until the old man swore the air blue or patted her sleek hide in an unwelcome spot, he chuckled inwardly. That should take care of Mrs. Bauman's social aspirations with the Power family. That and Ruby.

His eyes found Ruby in the middle of the room, surrounded by an admiring gaggle of printers from the atelier. He laughed out loud as he again admired her unparalleled choice of outfit for the Christmas party. The matron standing before him flushed happily, thinking she'd said something witty and clever.

She talked on, encouraged by his unexpected response. Jacques narrowed his eyes and studied the deep vee of Ruby's gold lamé bodice. If she bent over for any reason, there would be a riot. That is, if she *could* bend over without causing an irreparable rent up the back seam of her dress. He doubted the law of physics would allow such a move. Even the old man had been speechless for once when Ruby removed the red fox cape that protected her from the attention of any member of the vice squad who might catch a glimpse of her on the street. And Patrick Power considered himself a connoisseur of Ruby's chorus-line type of appeal. In this case the apple had certainly fallen far from the tree, Jacques mused. His own skin crawled when he contemplated the wild tendrils of glossy black hair snaking down her bare back, the slash of frosted gold eye shadow whose hue exactly matched the dress she wore like spray-enamel. He smiled again. Merry Christmas, Celia Bauman, he thought to himself. Celia would never know all the trouble he had undergone to find the perfect "date" for her snobby little soiree. Even in Manhattan, the city where almost anything could be found for a price, it had been difficult to engage a model as… colorful as Ruby. He chuckled at his little joke. Mrs. Bauman's friends, sprinkled not so discreetly throughout the room—he'd give them something beside the catering to talk about.

He was aware that Vanessa VanderPoel had arrived. He watched the butler help her out of a black wool coat at the front door. No, she was not the type to wear fur. She inclined her head and smiled at something the man said, the blond streaks of her hair catching the light as she did so. Now there was a woman with taste and breeding, a woman the old man would think was about as appealing as a piece of Steuben glass, if he even knew what Steuben glass was. Her pale gray dress, deceivingly demure at the collar, nevertheless flowed with her legs as she walked and made a man's hands long to caress the fine long thighs beneath the perfectly cut silk.

He drifted away from the woman at his side and slowly made his way across the room, angling toward the bar where he assumed she would head first. She radiated a special self-assurance in this group, a combination of the graceful and the authoritative, an unusual mixture in a woman her age, which he assumed to be around thirty. But most people felt more confident with a glass as a prop in their hands at a large gathering and he knew she would probably arrive at the bar shortly after he did. He waited with his back leaning casually on the bar, ignoring the offer of a refill from the bartender and watching her greet various guests at the party. She allowed Celia Bauman to kiss the air at either side of her high and angular cheekbones. At last she was looking in his direction and their eyes locked. A becoming blush crept over her cheeks, so lightly and smoothly that she might have suddenly acquired a slight sunburn. Her eyes, as she looked into his, seemed to be the intense, clear blue of the Baltic Sea, the cold northern waters off the coast of Scandinavia. Her name was Dutch, he remembered, but Viking blood flowed in those veins, he was certain. A friendly greeting touched her lips, yet the cool eyes measured him even as the face smiled.

"Jacques, nice to see you. How strange we haven't run into each other at the atelier."

Strange indeed, he thought. *You know I've been avoiding you.* She had disturbed him curiously that night at her apartment. He took one of her hands and surprised himself by kissing the back of it, intensely aware of the fine blue lines spidered beneath the translucent skin. A kinetic energy seemed to flow between her fine hand and his powerful one.

"Here alone? I would imagine that a beautiful woman like you never lacks for an escort. Where's the man with the bathrobe?" Even as he spoke, he knew she was not beautiful in the classic sense. But she exuded an air of regal sensuality he had never before encountered. Her eyes held a secret, a sad undercurrent of compassion he had seldom seen in the women he knew. She laughed and answered as if she *did* guard a secret.

"He's here. I'll introduce you if your curiosity is that great." She looked around the room quickly. He studied her profile as she turned her head away from him. Great planes, he thought, a vision of Cezanne-like angles blurring the varicolored background of the party.

"I don't care to meet him. Would you like a drink?"

"I'd just like a wine spritzer, but, knowing Celia, I'll probably have to 'settle' for a Dom Pérignon."

"Exactly." He turned and ordered for them both. "Is Celia a friend of yours?" he asked as they waited for two glasses of champagne. "Why all this display of wealth?"

"Reaction, I guess. I'm not close to Celia, but I know she comes from a very poor, very strict family. Her father was a minister in one of those sects that doesn't permit cards or music or dancing on Saturday night. I know Richard much better. He's been a good friend to me."

"Have you worked for him long?"

"Ever since I got out of art school eight years ago."

"You wanted to be an artist?" He was surprised. She was not what he considered the creative type.

"Yes, does that surprise you?" When he did not respond immediately, she asked him, "Why? Don't you believe in women artists?" He thought she was a shade defensive in her quick question.

"It's not that." He chose his words carefully. "You seem to be so meticulous, so self-contained. Not that those qualities preclude a career in art. But it is hard for a woman to make it in the art world. There *are* no contemporary female artists of note, you know."

"Oh? What about Nevelson and O'Keeffe?"

"Name two more, if you can," he challenged.

"Helen Frankenthaler and.."

"And who? You see, you can't do it. So, what happened? From artist to chromist is quite a step—"

"Quite a step down? Is that what you were going to say?" she asked quickly.

"Not if I could bite my tongue fast enough," he grinned sheepishly. "I didn't mean it to sound quite so condescending." His quick apology surprised even himself. For some reason he did not want to offend this woman. Usually he didn't think twice about what he said or to whom. Long ago he had learned that his fame and talent shielded him from the necessities of conventional behavior. That, in fact, he was often expected to be eccentric, even if that sometimes translated into being offensive. And he knew that this lack of inhibition in him frequently intimidated others, effectively protecting his internal need for privacy. But he wanted this coolly appraising Scandinavian princess to look on him with benevolence, even to approve of him. God, what had come over him? He hadn't curried the approval of anyone since he had been a child. Since he had learned the hard way that the only thing that counted in South Boston was the muscle behind your closed fists—not your talent, not your sensitivity, not your aspirations to get out of the Irish ghetto by sheer hard work. He could never expect this pampered woman to understand. She looked like she'd been raised by an English nanny. Just the way her tapered fingers held the thin stem of the champagne glass. No nail polish, he liked that. Sleekly groomed, but not artificial. Except for the hair—those streaks were too perfect to be natural.

"Why did you want to be an artist?" He was genuinely interested. She was a study in contradiction, he realized and suddenly he had a desire to know much more about her. She was unlike the first impression he'd had of her in Bauman's office. Her apartment, for instance, the opposite of what he had assumed it would be. That air she had around her. She appeared so self-assured, so glacial, that he had wanted to stick a pin in her placid exterior. And he'd done so very effectively, he realized later in the deli. She'd acted totally nonplussed at their meeting there. Her confused behavior had satisfied him, but it had also strangely endeared her to him and had made him want to atone for his boorish behavior earlier.

"I used to think I had some talent. My father was the art critic on a Cleveland newspaper and he encouraged me. However, when I got into the major leagues here in New York, I realized I'd been mistaken. But I had good color sense, a good technical background. Richard took me on and trained me as a chromist. I've never regretted it. I make a decent living." She spoke with simple self-honesty, as if she were summing up the attributes of a third party. He enjoyed her candor. So many women felt they had to come on to him strongly, as if to prove they were worthy of his attention. She wasn't putting herself down but she wasn't trying to impress him either.

"Are you here alone?" she asked him unexpectedly. She was looking at him in a funny way. He realized he must have been staring.

"My father's here. And I brought a, um, a date." Against his will his eyes went to the middle of the room where Ruby still held court. Vanessa's eyes followed the path his had taken. For an instant her ice-blue pupils widened, but then her face composed itself smoothly, almost as if she had lowered a curtain. He saw a look he could not read in her eyes.

"If you'll excuse me, I see someone I should say hello to." She moved away from him without a further word. He watched her trim legs as she made her way across the crowded room. God, what a cool customer. He knew women well. He'd never had any trouble summing them up, knowing just how far he could go without getting his face slapped. Sometimes he felt he could literally read their minds. But this Vanessa was different. Jacques knew there was something between the two of them, that special irrational electricity that leaps between a man and a woman with no forewarning, the literal bolt from the blue. He'd felt it the first time he saw her. And if she wasn't experiencing the same fibrillation, then everything he'd learned about women in his forty years was in error. When he had kissed her that night in her apartment, he'd been sure she was as aroused as he, but she'd turned him down flat. He had been astonished at his unwonted miscalculation—and a bit wounded, totally unprepared for her firm rejection. He'd gone out of his way to avoid her since that night, figuring that there were plenty more fish in the sea. But just when he thought he had put her out of his mind, she had entered the same elevator he was already riding. She had not seen him, seemingly engrossed as she was in a memo she held in her delicate hand. He had smelled the sweet fragrance of her hair, redolent of lilies of the valley, and wanted to slip his arms around her and bury his head in her neck. Wanted to start again with her, with more patience and tenderness, and penetrate the mysterious shell that surrounded her.

She was talking to the curator from the atelier—what was his name? Myron? Millard? And a well-dressed, dark-haired younger man. She slipped her arm through the curator's possessively and Jacques realized suddenly that he was the bathrobe man. She had said he was here at the party, even offered to introduce him. An alien jolt of fire shot through Jacques, an emotion he did not immediately recognize. The man was too old for Vanessa, he told himself. The curator's thinning hair declared that he must be near fifty, although the graying temples were distinguished. Jacques narrowed his eyes and appraised him: He was tall and thin and looked as if he valued a healthy body. His clothes were splendid, obviously expensive and tastefully chosen to hang perfectly on his well-proportioned shape. He appeared to be a cultured and educated man, so perhaps he was her type, after all. Jacques already knew Vanessa was an intelligent woman. In fact he was certain that behind those icy blue eyes there lurked plenty of brains. She didn't need to impress people with what she knew, just the knowing would be enough for her. And behind those icy blue eyes there lurked a fire that needed the right man to fan it to life. The curator was not that man, didn't she realize that?

Suddenly Jacques named the unfamiliar emotion—jealousy! He laughed at himself unbelievably.

Yes, he'd been impressed. Impressed enough to feel jealous of the way her hand rested on that man's arm, impressed enough to experience a twinge of pain when her lovely laugh reached his ears across the crowded room. He'd give her a little time and try again later. Wouldn't do to be too pushy with her—he'd learned that already, the hard way.

Bauman was bearing down on him. Jacques moved away from the bar to meet him. Poor guy, even from ten feet away, he saw a fine sheen of perspiration on Bauman's upper lip and high forehead.

"Jacques, did you get enough to eat? How about another drink? Help yourself. Celia has a fabulous caterer, one of the best in town, so she tells me."

"I'm fine, Richard. I want to talk to you about our contract." Jacques was not fond of business discussions outside of the shop. It wasn't that he was sorry to intrude on a social occasion, but he always worried that alcohol blurred people's judgment and memories. He'd learned to be cautious from living with his father. Tonight, however, he had to buttonhole Bauman; what he had to say he wanted held in confidence and Bauman never seemed to be alone at the atelier.

"Is there something wrong?" Nervous anguish jumped into Bauman's eyes. "Whatever it is, we can work—"

"Everything's all right, Bauman. Take it easy." Jacques had never met such a jumpy man. "I simply want to change the method of payment, that's all. We had talked about four equal sums at two-month intervals. I want the first two payments sent to the South Boston Boys Club. I want them sent anonymously, and I want them earmarked for college scholarships for the neediest of the boys who want to study the graphic arts."

"You don't want them to know the money's from you? What about tax deductions? What about the publicity—it'll be fabulous for your image, Jacques. I know just the P.R. man to handle it, really make it something in the press." Bauman rubbed his hands together energetically.

"I don't *want* any publicity, that's why I'm talking to you about it here instead of at the atelier. Anonymous means just that—anonymous. And as for the tax aspect, I'll let my accountant worry about that. Can you handle that for me? I mean, in the way I want it handled?"

"Well, sure, if that's really what you want," Bauman answered doubtfully. "You know, I'll do whatever you ask. But, I know this would make a great story."

"Listen, Bauman, I've been doing this for years and no one has ever known. If the word gets out now, I'll know that you are responsible for it, and I'll take appropriate action, if you get my drift." Jacques's hazel eyes seemed to cloud to a steely gray. There was menace in the low words.

"Yes, I understand. You mean, you do this all the time? What's in it for you?"

"Whenever I can. And why should there be something in it for me? I never got a single break when I was a kid. From the time I was about ten I knew I was going to be an artist and in the place I grew up you had to defend a decision like that with your fists every damn day of your life. Even my old man used to ask me if I was a pansy. Only one person had any faith in me—a teacher I had in the ninth grade. He helped me obtain a small scholarship to scrape by my first year in art college. If it weren't for the existence of some anonymous money, I'd still be loading freight. So I'm paying back the only way I know how. That's what's in it for me."

Bauman looked at him with renewed respect. "Don't

worry, your secret's safe with me. I'll take care of the papers tomorrow, myself. No one will know. Have you met everyone? Do you know the lady in the purple suit? She's with *Women's Wear Daily* and I know she's been dying to meet you.'' Jacques groaned inwardly as Bauman propelled him by the elbow toward a hawk-faced woman engaged in conversation with the bejeweled Celia.

He looked over his shoulder toward Vanessa, wondering how to get back to her.

Chapter Four

He really *was* an animal, after all, Vanessa told herself
with disgust. With great effort she kept her eyes
averted from the wriggling gold lamé spectacle who
dispensed sexual innuendo and musk perfume to the
appreciative group of boisterous men surrounding
her. If she could just reach Maynard and his friend,
Vanessa would feel safe, would feel as if she had re-
gained control once more. Right this minute she
verged on angry tears. She had not experienced such
an attack of naked jealousy since high school. And
back then the object of her jealousy, a pampered and
rich little brat from Gates Mills, had been a far wor-
thier opponent. She could feel Jacques's eyes on her
back as if they were shooting green flames. She would
not give him the satisfaction of seeing her turn her
head. She hoped the two dots of crimson anger on her
cheeks would be mistaken for cosmetics in the flattering light of the Baumans' luxurious living room.

"There you are, my dear. We saw you come in, but
Power got his hands on you first." Maynard kissed
her with exaggerated European courtesy on either

cheek. "Meet my friend, Antonio da Silva, decorator extraordinaire, and newest pet of the South American parvenus."

"A pleasure, Mr. da Silva." His soft hand took hers and he leaned over it gracefully, feigning a polite continental kiss. His sartorial splendor impressed even Vanessa, although she had grown accustomed to Maynard's sometimes incredible flights of fancy in costume.

"Antonio is just back from Manzanillo where he has been bringing some style to condominiums at Las Hadas, the fairy-tale resort on the Pacific. He is from the Dominican Republic and he's terribly talented, my dear, but terribly." Maynard gave the dark man a fond glance, which was warmly reciprocated.

"I believe you did mention his Mexican project to me, Maynard." She asked Antonio about his clients and his approach and, by allowing him to do most of the talking, found the ability to compose herself. She pointedly kept her back to Power, although a strange new radar told her where Jacques stood in the room at all times. She accepted a second glass of champagne when Da Silva detained a waiter who passed them bearing a silver tray of bubbling glasses in his hands. She began to feel bold and extravagant and seductive, although she knew her eyes sparkled brightly and her musical laugh carried across the room for Jacques and not for the two men who regaled her appreciative ears with cynical gossip of the foibles of the rich. It was with a sense of careless abandon that she acquiesced when Maynard suggested inviting Jacques and his father back to his apartment for a pickup dinner.

"Go ahead," she urged him, recklessly. "He'll never accept. Although you need a person like that woman to knock the stuffing out of your doorman. He thinks the only people who should be permitted to enter your building are the ones in *Burke's Peerage*."

"But, my dear, naturally *she* will not be included in the invitation. And if I could avoid the father as well, I would most certainly do so. However, I suppose he *is* the lesser of two evils." Maynard's nose wrinkled with unspoken distaste. She watched with a disbelieving smile on her lips as he crossed the room and broke into a conversation between Jacques and a middle-aged woman in purple chiffon. She still thought Maynard was joking until she saw Jacques's eyes crinkle with pleasure and his head nod in her direction. The faint smile faded from her lips and a cold ball of panic welled up from the pit of her stomach.

"Maynard, you're serious! What are you doing?" She attacked him upon his return to her side.

"I'm merely putting you on notice that you've been alone long enough. This Power is obviously of interest to you and you are to him. Neither of you seems to know just how to go about it, so I'm going to get you together."

"Oh, please. You're wrong! He really, really is not my type. Just *look* at that woman he brought here tonight. How could I be of interest to a man who would go around with a woman like her? How could he be of interest to *me*? Really, Maynard, this time you've gone too far. I won't go! I'm going home right this minute." Her eyes burned with anger at him.

"Vanessa, you're totally unreasonable. I can tell

from all my life experience, that cat woman means
nothing to him. Why, he hasn't looked her way once
tonight. I imagine he brought her just to shake up Celia. And bull's eye—she nearly had apoplexy when
they walked in. Now, get your coat like a good girl—
we'll be leaving in two minutes. Would you deprive
me of the opportunity to entertain Jacques Power in
my own apartment? Because if you don't come, he
won't.''

"Did he say that?" Her voice betrayed flattered interest, despite a desire to continue her tone of outrage
with Maynard.

"He asked if *Miss* VanderPoel would be there.
Doesn't he know about Andrew?"

"No, there was no reason to tell him. It's none of
his business, anyway."

"Ah, Antonio, you see we have our work cut out
for us this evening." He winked conspiratorially at Da
Silva, who smiled back in agreement. Maynard took
each of them by the elbow and propelled them toward
the door. "Jack shall have Jill; naught shall go ill," he
recited clearly as they made their way through the
crowd.

"Maynard, I want to powder my nose before we
leave." She needed a moment alone to compose herself. She was still highly uncertain about Maynard's
plan. Dear Maynard could be so obvious at times. She
was fond of him, true, but his machinations with
Jacques were apt to backfire in a most embarrassing
way. Vanessa hated to be manipulated by anyone,
even a well-intentioned friend. She entered Celia's
peach and mauve bedroom. Standing before an ornate

Art Deco mirror, she combed her shoulder-length hair and freshened her lipstick. In the mirror she watched the woman in gold lamé enter the room and cross to the bed where the women's coats lay.

So *she* was coming to Maynard's for dinner.

Suddenly Vanessa knew going to Maynard's was a mistake. How could she spend the balance of the evening looking at that woman with Jacques? She did not want to know another thing about him, about his life, about this woman. She snapped her black silk clutch bag shut with decision. Vanessa knew how to put him out of her mind and would. She'd been able to forget unpleasant—even tragic—events and get on with life. Certainly, she could forget *him*. This crazy obsession had to come to an end! After all, nothing of consequence had taken place between her and Jacques. How easy it would be to forget him. She'd find Maynard right now and tell him she had a headache, tell him she just remembered another date. Whatever she thought up, Maynard would object, but there was nothing he could do to stop her once she made up her mind.

Vanessa returned to the front hall carrying her coat. Maynard and Antonio were nowhere to be seen. Only Jacques stood there alone, holding his coat and lounging against a Chinese chest that sat before a mirrored wall.

"Where has everyone gone?" she asked Jacques with surprise.

"They've gone on to what's-his-name's to get supper ready. He's been inviting people left and right. He wanted me to wait for you, to bring you up to his place. I told him that would be all right with you."

She decided to ignore his unwarranted assumption that she would allow a virtual stranger to make her decisions. Oh, she'd been had by a master, she knew it. Maynard had anticipated her cold feet and fixed the arrangements so she would be unable to withdraw. No, not unable, but unwilling to withdraw.

"And your father, where is he?"

"He took Ruby down to find her a cab."

"Ruby? Ruby of the golden eyelids?" She tried to keep the malice from her voice, but he heard the note of disdain clearly. Ruby in another cab, alone.

"The very same. Didn't you care for her make-up?" His eyes were laughing, waiting for her to answer. She decided to choose her words carefully. It wouldn't do for him to know how battered she had actually felt when first she realized he had come to the party with Ruby. Ruby, what a perfect name! Maybe she *would* go to Maynard's party after all. Jacques did not seem put out that he'd been asked to wait for her. If anything, he appeared to be pleased by the turn of events.

"She was—what shall I say? She was memorable." Vanessa tried to laugh lightly.

"I think we can both say 'memorable' and I think we ought to say nothing else about the subject." Jacques appeared uncomfortable, a surprise to Vanessa, considering his usual cool and sardonic manner. "Shall we go?"

He helped her on with her coat. She thought his hands lingered on her shoulders a second longer than was necessary. He put on his own coat, the honey-colored sheepskin she had seen him wear before. He was dressed casually in a beige corduroy suit and a brown and tan plaid wool tie, just what she would expect Jacques to wear to a party where everyone else was in holiday finery.

"You don't care what anyone thinks of you, do you?" she asked him as they left the attended elevator.

"Certainly, I do. I care what some people think. Not too many, though. In an ideal situation, I'd like to be judged on my work, but that's a desire you can seldom fulfill in the real world. Some of the people at that party, for instance—they know my name and that I'm a big gun in art, but if you asked them to pick out one of my paintings, they wouldn't be able to tell mine from an Andy Warhol soup can."

"That's a little harsh, don't you think? After all it's the public that makes a market for your work."

"No, it's the media that makes the market, not public taste—if the phrase 'public taste' isn't a contradiction in terms all by itself."

"Oh, my, you really do look down on the average man. I thought you prided yourself on your humble beginnings."

"Come on, Vanessa, you know better than that. In art school you must have met scores of students who were as good as I am—better maybe. The world is full of potentially good artists. Some of us get the breaks, that's all. A lucky few are taken up by the press, get known as the darlings of the art world, become famous and rich. There's hardly a correlation between talent and success, more's the pity." All this time he had been looking up Fifth Avenue in search of an empty taxi. She was studying the strong lines of his

jaw and the creases around his eyes when he turned
and caught her staring.

"What are you staring at?"

"You," she replied simply.

"What's so interesting now?"

"You're not what you seem, what you want others
to think you are. It must be quite hard work to keep
up that glowering image, Jacques. Why don't you simply be yourself? Life is easier when you are."

"That's garbage and you know it," he answered
gruffly. "We're never going to find a taxi here," he
said quickly, changing the subject. An invisible barrier
seemed to drop between them.

"Let's walk. Maynard's place is only ten blocks
from here. It's a nice night." She allowed him to draw
her arm through his and they fell into step, heading
uptown. She was barely aware of the sedately twinkling white lights proclaiming the season with under-
stated elegance in the spindly limbs of the trees along
Fifth Avenue. She could only feel the warmth that
seeped into her at the hard nearness of his body to
hers. She shivered in pleasure at his closeness, aware
that too much time had passed since she had reacted
with desire for a man.

"Are you cold? Maybe walking isn't such a good
idea. I'll find a taxi if you like." His voice was gentle,
solicitous.

"No, not at all. And I can use the exercise after all
those delicious hors d'oeuvres at the Baumans'." She
pulled herself imperceptibly closer to him.

"I'm not hungry, are you? We could skip your
friend's place and go somewhere else. After all, the

only reason I was going was to see you, and you're with me now." He stopped and turned to face her. He removed a glove and stuffed it into the pocket of his jacket. He lifted her left hand and peeled off her glove. She looked down at her bare hand in his.

"Where did you have in mind?" She already knew what he was going to say. "Your place?"

"My place," he said at the same instant. They laughed at the same moment too. Her laugh was thin and nervous. She wanted to go with him. Wanted to grasp his wild red hair in her fingers and draw his head to her breast. She could not lift her eyes from the sight of her hand in his.

"And what about Ruby?" Her voice seemed to come from far away. But she had to know if Ruby was a part of Jacques's life. If another woman was on the scene, so to speak. She knew she was hopelessly old-fashioned. She knew that people weren't supposed to worry about other relationships these days. She knew. But she could not help herself. She told herself that he had a right to his life, just as she did to hers. She was aware that an invitation to his loft was not a proposal of marriage and implied nothing except that he desired her and that he recognized the same raw urge in her. She knew all those things, but she held her breath as she waited for his answer. After a too-long silence she looked up into his eyes.

"Ruby?" He repeated the name with an uncomprehending look on his face. "Oh, Ruby! Don't worry about her—she won't be there, if that's what you mean." He hooted with laughter. Vanessa didn't see any humor in the subject.

"Who is she?" she asked.

"Ruby's a model."

"Who does she model for, Frederick's of Hollywood?" Vanessa's cheeks were burning with embarrassment. Why was he laughing at her? She was suddenly very angry, more at herself for considering his invitation than at his unexpected hoot of enjoyment. People on the street were turning to stare.

"No, she's an artist's model. Never a lack of work for Ruby." His eyes were crinkled with laughter.

"*You* don't use a model. I've seen your work—it's all abstract."

"You never know when someone like Ruby will come in handy. Come to think of it, I don't think she models for anyone. She just likes to be known as a model. Look, here's a cab. Are you coming or not?"

"I can see all your etchings at the atelier. I think I'll pass." At Jacques's signal the taxi stopped in front of them. He yanked open the door and pushed Vanessa into the backseat. He climbed in behind her.

"SoHo," he said curtly to the driver.

"Wait a minute. I want to go home, or at least I want to go to Mayn—" He covered her mouth with his large hand.

"You can't seriously think I'd be so trite as to ask you up to see my etchings. I want to show you the real thing, the originals." His face was very close to her and his whispered breath lay warm on her cheek. She looked at him with wide open eyes. She knew his words were an attempt to make light of the situation, but the look in his hazel eyes caused a tingle to run through her limbs. There was purpose and intensity

in his face. His casual words belied the need she read
in his somber eyes. Even though he exuded power
and insolence and a devil-may-care attitude to the
world, she sensed a part of Jacques, deep within his
core, that reached out for tenderness. For some un-
fathomable reason, he had chosen to protect this hidden vulnerability from the world. His naked need
struck a chord of response within her breast. She
longed to reach out to him, to touch his inner soul.
They looked into one another's eyes for a long moment.

Finally, when she could no longer bear the haunted
look she read in the depths of his eyes, she closed her
own and nodded her head in assent, so slightly that
she wondered if he had seen. But he saw or felt her
nod. He removed his hand from where it covered her
mouth and slipped it behind her head, pulling her
mouth to his in a rough kiss. His lips were hard and
demanding and she felt her own open under their insistent pressure, admitting his tongue. Timidly she
touched her tongue to his and felt his answering arms
increase the power of his embrace. He crushed her to
him in an endless kiss. A languid warmth stole
through her bones and weakened her to the point of
trembling. When at last he drew his head away and
she opened her eyes to look into his, she expected to
see a gleam of triumph in their green depths. But what
she saw was a new and unexpected glow of tenderness
and concern for her, which surprised her more than
anything else that had transpired that evening.

Jacques took her chin and tilted it up so that she
could not avoid his serious eyes.

"You won't be sorry, Vanessa." The hoarseness of passion muffled his somber voice. "I won't hurt you. I promise you that."

He did not attempt to kiss her again, nor did they speak on the long ride downtown. Instead, he grasped her ungloved hand and tucked it firmly under his arm, as if to imprison her in case she decided to change her mind again. She glanced at his rugged profile from time to time, but when her sporadic breathing had returned to a near-normal rhythm, she too sat in stillness and gazed out the window at the reflection of the street lights speeding by. Her mind dwelt, for the first of many, many times to come, on the unexpected words he had mumbled.

A strange calm seemed to have settled over Jacques, a calm so complete it was as if he had already spent himself making love to her. With a sinking heart she wondered if the chase was everything to this man. Perhaps confronted with her submission, he was losing interest. She could pretend that she was as calm as he and she did, her chin held high as she stared unseeingly out the window, but in reality she was a clutch of nerves, her body held tightly in trembling awareness of the closeness of his hard maleness next to her on the narrow seat. From time to time he squeezed her hand quickly, wordlessly assuring her not to worry, and she would forget the hesitation that nagged still.

He wrapped his arms around her and buried his head in her neck during the slow, clanking elevator ride up to the studio loft. Not a word was spoken as he unlocked the door and turned on the overhead spotlights, illuminating a cavernous space—part studio, part living quarters—which filled an entire floor of the building. Finished and partly finished canvases leaned against all the visible walls. Their footsteps echoed as they entered the partition-divided room.

"Did you see the woman outside?" she asked him as he took her coat.

"No, I didn't notice. Why?"

But of course there was no way to tell him without admitting to him that she had been here before and had seen the same woman in front. "Oh, I just wonder why she would be standing out there on such a cold night."

"She's probably waiting for someone. Anyway, the neighborhood's filled with all sorts of oddballs, just like all the rest of New York. Are you hungry?"

"Shall I cook you something? Show me the kitchen," she said, surprised at herself for offering. But something in her wanted to take care of Jacques and it seemed right to offer to cook for him.

"I'm starving," he answered. "*You* can take care of everything." He took her by the elbow and led her around a partition behind an easel on which an enormous, half-painted canvas rested.

"But this is the bedroom!" She giggled. She was beginning to understand the little boy who emerged from time to time in his complex personality.

"Who said anything about food? Man can't live by bread alone." He threw his jacket on a chair and loosened his tie with one hand as he turned on a soft light next to a queen-size bed with the other. "Do you want a drink, though? You seem keyed up. Are you nervous?"

"No," she lied. She wanted to be as nonchalant as he, although it was not in her character to take him as lightly as he seemed to take himself. She removed her earrings and laid them on a small chest next to the bed. Her fingers trembled. She began to undress, fumbling with the cuff buttons of the gray silk dress.

"Please, let me," he said very quietly. He was at her side. She smelled a new scent on him, an aroma of exotic wood, and she knew it was the scent of desire. His large fingers easily manipulated the buttons. He placed his hand on her shoulder and turned her around so that he could open the zipper of the dress. He turned her around again and kissed her slowly and tenderly. She undid the buttons of his shirt and pushed back the sleeves to reveal the hard muscles of his neck and arms. She buried her face in the mat of red hair she discovered on his chest.

"A natural redhead," she joked.

"I promised you the real thing," he answered as he slipped her dress down and kissed the cleft between her breasts. She heard her own sharp intake of breath. The dress fell to the floor at their feet and she stepped gracefully out of it. He backed her toward the bed and her knees gave way as her legs met its edge. Soon they were lying together on the bed, his hands pushing her slip down to her waist and his lips closing over the hardened nipples of her breasts, caressing first one, then the other.

"You are beautiful, my princess, my Scandinavian princess. I want you so badly."

The slip was on the floor and she lay with her eyes closed and listened to the rustle of fabric when he stood to remove the rest of his clothes. He returned to her side and stretched his muscular body next to hers on the coverlet. Without the protective covering of clothing his lean body betrayed a background of heavy work. To her surprise muscles bulged in his shoulders and forearms. She touched his hard chest in pleased delight. Renewed tremors of desire quivered within her when he gently removed what little remained of her underclothes and she found herself naked beneath his gaze. She opened her eyes at the sound of his appreciative intake of breath. With his head propped on one hand, his intense hazel eyes looked into hers for a long, silent moment before he leaned down and covered her neck, her breasts, and her stomach with his warm kisses. She arched her body to his in unconscious desire to be as close to him as possible, to become a part of him.

His large hands stroked the smooth curves of her body, lingering on the fullness of her breasts, descending slowly to her stomach, and coming to rest between her thighs. At the same time his lips were buried in the hollow of her throat. Instinctively she twisted her fingers in his wiry red hair and pulled his head closer to her. She barely knew where his body ended and hers began. Incongruous thoughts floated through her head. How unusual was the texture of his skin, how unlike any skin she had ever touched. She silently chided herself for worrying that she would not know what to do. Making love was like riding a bicycle, she told herself irreverently—one never forgets. Although, it had been a long time since she and Andrew.... She felt disloyal to Andrew for wanting

Jacques more than she had ever wanted her husband. And she felt disloyal to Jacques for allowing the thought of Andrew to enter her head. But Andrew was the only man she had ever known and each sensation she experienced with Jacques was so unlike anything she had felt with her husband, she could not help comparing. She was afraid she might say Andrew's name.

But soon the compelling fullness of intense desire arose in her and she returned Jacques's kisses and caresses, heedless of her former fear of the volatile artist in her arms and unmindful of her previous life with Andrew. She covered his neck and shoulders with urgent kisses of her own, reveling in the exotic taste of his skin on her tongue. She moaned in response to the gentle fondling of his hands. She allowed her hands to glide over his hard body with an easy familiarity and enjoyed the sound of each groan of response in his throat. Although each sensation had the excitement and clarity of newness with him, at the same time she felt as if they had made love a hundred times already, that he knew as instinctively as she exactly what would bring the other the most pleasure. She turned to him and whispered his name one time. At her signal, he covered her body with his. They hesitated for another moment, looking deeply into each other's hungry eyes, knowing that the pain of waiting just a small moment longer would intensify the ultimate pleasure of their union.

"Boyooo—are y'here?" a man shouted.

"Oh, my God, who's that?" Vanessa pulled away from Jacques in agonized surprise. Her legs went weak with shock. The voice called again, so close he seemed to be in the same room with them.

"My father!" Jacques rolled to his back and swore roundly. "What the hell is *he* doing here?" He swore again, this time in words Vanessa had never heard strung together so colorfully.

"Is that what they taught you on the docks?" She attempted to laugh lightly through the tears of sudden frustration that welled up in her eyes and caused the whispered words to catch in her throat, but she could not. "Is he coming in here? There aren't any doors! Oh, Jacques—stop him!"

"That s.o.b., he's supposed to be at your friend's for dinner. And listen, he's not alone."

Vanessa wasn't listening. She scrambled as fast as possible under the covers of the bed and pulled the sheets up to her chin. She eyed her silk dress lying in a discarded heap on the floor. The dress seemed to be at least a hundred feet away from where she lay. Jacques jumped from the bed and pulled on his pants.

"Just a minute," he called out. "Stay right where you are! I'll be out in a minute." He turned and whispered to her. "I'll keep him busy. Better put your clothes on—there aren't any doors, you're right. I've never needed any before." His voice was low, but his green eyes were hard with anger.

He left the bedroom area. She jumped up and dressed with cold and trembling hands. She ran a comb through her hair and quickly checked her makeup in a mirror. Her lips were swollen with the passion of Jacques's kisses. How was she ever going to escape from his loft without seeing the group of people she could hear arriving? She listened to Jacques's and his father's voices speaking on the other side of the partition, Jacques's angry and his father's defensive, but she was unable to make out their words. At last Jacques returned and threw on his shirt and shoes, mumbling under his breath all the time.

"He's brought a bunch of people back from the party," he told her. "And not only that, he stopped at the local tavern and picked up some of his drinking buddies. God, I can't stand the idea of those rummies in my studio! What the hell's the matter with him, anyway? He never cared, never gave a damn about me and my work." He sat dejectedly on the side of the bed.

"Jacques, people from the party here? Now? You mean the printers from the atelier?" She sat down next to him on the bed. He lifted one of her hands in his and stroked it absently. She put an arm around his neck and whispered in his ear, "I don't want to see anyone from the office, Jacques, you can understand that. How can we get out of here? We could go back to my apartment. Isn't there another way out? Please, you have to help me."

"I can't, oh, God, I can't." She was startled to see the pain in his eyes.

"You can't? You mean there's no other way out?"

"No. I mean yes. There's another door down the back stairs. I mean that I can't go back to your place. God, I want to go with you!" He wrapped his arms tightly around her and held her in silence. "There's nothing in the world I want to do more than be with you now. But how can I leave that bunch of drunks here in my studio? Just listen to them!''

Vanessa knew he was right. Loud music was already blaring from an unseen stereo. She heard shouts of gay laughter and the clink of glasses. More people seemed to be arriving every minute.

"Can't you stay, Vanessa?" Even as he asked they both knew that for her to stay was impossible. "No, never mind, I know you can't. They'll be here all night, I suppose. Damn!"

"What are *you* going to do?" she asked him.

"What can I do? Just protect my canvases and hope that no one gets in a fist fight or decides to try his hand at painting. I'm so sorry. Let me take you downstairs and find you a cab."

"Jacques, *I'm* sorry. I want to be with you, you know that, don't you? I just couldn't face—"

"Yes, I know. Anyway, I wouldn't want you to see my old man in action first hand. You might get the wrong impression of me." He laughed bitterly. "Just stay here, I'll get the coats. I'll be right back."

She sat on the edge of the bed and waited. She heard footsteps return in a moment, but when she looked up, not Jacques but his father came into the sleeping area, his arms laden with coats, which he threw on the bed at her side. Vanessa jumped to her feet.

"So here's the little lady all hidden away! Come out and have a drink, join the party." He swayed unsteadily on his feet. "Hope we didn't interrupt anything." He winked knowingly at her. She felt a blush begin at her breasts and rise immediately to color her face.

"I was just leaving, Mr. Power."

"Ah, you know my name, but I haven't had the pleasure, pretty lady." He came around the bed and extended his hand to her. Automatically she shook his hand, but she had no intention of giving him her name.

"I'm just a good friend of your son's."

"A very *good* friend of his, it seems. You're a nice-looking filly." His words slurred and the smell of alcohol impelled Vanessa to step back quickly. She lost her footing and sat suddenly on the bed once more. Her hands felt the silky touch of fur and she looked down to see she sat on a red fox cape. She snatched her hand away.

"Whose coat is this?" She laid her hand on the fur once more. It was an effort to keep it from trembling.

As if on cue, Ruby walked into the bedroom area.

"Let me have that. I'll just hang it up." Ruby lifted the fox and shook it before crossing the room in tiny steps, her progress impeded by the tightness of her dress. She opened a sliding door Vanessa hadn't noticed and hung the fox cape next to Jacques's shirts. "My little baby needs a place to sleep too," she crooned and left the room, musk trailing behind her unsteady steps.

"She seems to know her way around," said Vanessa through the pain of realizing that the woman Jacques had pretended to ignore knew just where the bedroom closet was.

"Sure, she does. She's been around. My son has interesting friends." He tottered on the balls of his feet as he eyed Vanessa appreciatively.

"And *she'll* need a place to sleep too?" *Please give me the right answer,* she begged him silently.

"She sleeps right here," he stated, patting the bed.

Vanessa found the strength to stand. Oh, how could she have been so naive as to think Ruby hadn't slept in this bed often? She looked around the room for some sign of Ruby's presence in the loft—a discarded garment, a half-used bottle of musk scent on the dresser. The room blurred. She thought she might faint.

"You look sick," slurred Jacques's father. "I'll be getting you a brandy. That'll take care of what ails you, my pretty." He squeezed her arm and left the room quickly.

She closed her eyes in misery. She had believed him! How she'd ached to believe that Ruby was no one to Jacques. Why, Ruby might have come in and found them making love, found them naked in this bed together. *Her* bed! Vanessa wanted to be gone, to be alone in the silence of her own apartment. Why had she been so blind? Why had she ignored Maynard's warning about Jacques? No, she had allowed Jacques to turn her head, had allowed her own need for him to blot out all the warning signals. *Oh, what a fool I've been!* She picked up her purse and was ready when at length Jacques returned with their coats.

He led her to a stairwell in the back of the loft. They saw no one in the passage. Silently they descended the narrow stairway together, she trying to not touch him as they negotiated the steep, iron steps. She concentrated on putting one foot in front of the other. How could he have deceived her so? She was furious—at him, of course, but more so at herself for grasping at

the line he'd tossed her. What *had* he said exactly?
She no longer remembered his actual words but the
words didn't matter. Her first impression had been
right all along: He was just a conceited playboy who
loved no one but himself.

"I'll call you tomorrow," he said gently, opening
the door of the taxi that came at his shrill whistle. He
put his arms around her but she stepped back out of
his reach.

"Don't bother," she answered.

He grasped her wrist and pulled her to him, his eyes
looking into hers with challenge. "What is this? Some
kind of teen-age game?"

"No game. I don't want to see you again, that's
all." She averted her head to avoid the hurt look in
his perplexed green eyes. "Don't call. There's nothing between us."

"What the hell are you saying? Look, I'm sorry I
can't come with you. I thought you understood—I
can't just simply walk out and leave them to wreck my
studio! Vanessa, what's going on?"

"I understand—*everything*! Now, if you will let go
of my arm, you're hurting me. I want to go home."

"Let her go, buddy. It's cold out there," said the
cab driver around the wet cigar clenched in his teeth.

"Shut up and mind your own business!"

"Good night, Jacques. Thanks for the tour of your
studio." She broke free of his grasp and threw herself
in the backseat of the taxi, giving the driver her address. Jacques forced his head and shoulders into the
car and the glower of rage that clouded his features
filled her with real fear.

"I don't play games, little girl," he hissed in low and distinct words. "When you're ready to be a real woman, come and see me again. Don't think I'll come to you!" With that he slammed the back door so hard the abused chassis of the taxi rattled ominously.

"Don't say a word," she snapped to the driver. "And put out that damned cigar!"

"Yes, ma'am." He dropped the shift into first gear and roared away from the curb. Vanessa did not look back. She knew the sidewalk was empty behind her.

Chapter Five

Once inside the sanctuary of her apartment she began to tremble. She felt cold all over—her very limbs ached with the cold. She did something she had never done before; she poured herself a generous glass of brandy and took it with her to bed. She wanted to stay in bed for a week. Strange, she had not felt this bereft since Andrew died. Her heart was suddenly empty, an empty vacuum. She knew with a sudden clarity that somewhere the gods had written that she was to be alone for all the days of her life. All the days, she said to herself—like an indeterminate sentence to prison the years stretched endlessly before her. Not the *rest* of her life, not *the duration* of her life. But *all the days*. How sad and final. She thought of the elderly Miss Weissman next door with a notice of whom to call if she were found dead pasted on the foyer mirror in her apartment. Tears welled up in her eyes and rolled down her cheeks unheeded. Jacques had seemed so different at the Baumans' party, not at all the brusque and rude man she had first met. And then later, at his loft, when they had begun to make love... Even now her body longed for what had been denied. With an audible moan she realized she would like nothing better than to be lying in his sinewy arms this very moment.

She knew Maynard was right about a lot of things. He *had* been right about Jacques, after all. But he wasn't right about everything. For a long time now he'd been telling her to take a risk, to remake her life, to become involved with another man. She couldn't—she just couldn't! She was terrified of being hurt again, simply immobilized by a fear of giving her heart away and having another man step all over it. Hadn't she just made an attempt with Jacques? And look what had happened. At least the ax had fallen quickly. Oh, the form the pain took was different with Jacques Power, but the suffering felt the same.

That woman, Ruby! She shook her head. How could she seriously have considered starting an affair with a man who found a person like Ruby attractive? Artist's model, indeed. "I'm not *that* desperate," she said aloud and was surprised by the nasal tone of her voice to find she had been crying. She reached for a tissue to blow her nose just as the telephone on the bedside table rang.

Her hand went back and forth in the space between the instrument and her bed. If it was Maynard, he would want a plausible excuse for her desertion. Could she say she was getting a cold? Certainly her teary voice would give some credence to the lie. And if it was Jacques— Her pulse began to hammer in her ears. What would she say? She was angry all right, and she had every right to be. And yet . . .

She lifted the receiver slowly and put it to her ear. She heard the tinny whine of a long-distance line.

"Vanessa, are you there?"

"Oh, Dad, what a surprise!" She tried to put animation in her words to cover the disappointment she felt. She listened attentively as he told her he would be passing through New York on his way home from a Christmas Caribbean cruise.

"I've been trying to get you for hours. My plane to Miami leaves tonight to meet the boat and I wanted to talk to you before. I have something exciting to tell you—at least I think it's exciting and I hope you will, too."

"I've been out—out at a Christmas party. A party at Jacques Power's studio." She found herself shading the truth because of a new, perverse need to say Jacques's name out loud to another person. Of course her father knew of Jacques's work and was suitably impressed that she was acquainted with him.

"A very kind man," her father said unexpectedly.

"Jacques Power, a kind man? You have to be kidding!"

"No, not at all. Before I retired I did a long article about Power for the Sunday supplement of the newspaper. I dug up a lot of interesting information about him, information that ultimately we weren't permitted to use. His lawyers stopped the publication of part of the piece, threatened us, actually. Since everything we had planned to say was complimentary, we decided to go along with their wishes. Good news doesn't sell papers, unfortunately. The public prefers to read scandalous garbage about their heroes any day."

"What kind of 'good news' do you mean?"

"Oh, the scholarships he funds, the donations to organizations in his old neighborhood, things like that. I have the clippings around somewhere and I'd be happy to send them to you if you like. But it will have to wait until I—I mean *we* return from the cruise."

"We? Do I hear a plural pronoun there?" she teased her father.

"You do, Vanessa. And you will, I hope, for a long time to come. I'm getting married. You may even know the bride. Her daughter went to school with you." He mentioned the name of a former classmate whom Vanessa barely remembered. She was unable to picture the girl's face let alone recall that of her mother.

"When is the happy occasion? I'd like to be there," she told him sincerely. He had been a widower for nearly twenty years. She could not imagine him as anyone's husband, not to mention the ardent suitor of a sixty-year-old woman. She knew it was unfair of her to categorize her father so, yet she could not help herself, unable to picture him in any role other than that of her sole parent. She became aware that she had missed something when she heard him say,

"... just a small wedding in Curaçao, no guests invited. Two of Marie's children live too far away to be able to attend a wedding in Cleveland, one other would not be able to afford to come, and the last one doesn't approve of the match to begin with. I hope *you* don't mind our arrangements. Rather than cause any hard feelings, we simply figured it would be easier all around if we came home and the marriage was a fait accompli. But I couldn't do that to you, Vanessa, I simply had to tell you my happy news."

"And I'm thrilled for you, Dad! You *should* be married; you *should* have someone to share your life with. You couldn't have given me a finer Christmas present than your news." Tears came to her eyes. She told herself they were tears of joy for him. But in her heart she felt a pang of fear that she too might be alone and lonely for twenty years before finding someone with whom to share her life. Or worse, that she might never find another.

"You'll find someone, dear," he said, somehow reading her thoughts from halfway across the country. "What about Power? Is he, ahem, eligible for consideration?"

"Dad! I hardly know the man. Besides, he's not my type. You must have discovered *that* aspect of his character in your research too."

"Ah, Vanessa, there's no explaining the attraction that springs up between people. History is made up of the most unlikely matches that worked."

"Well, I have no plans at the present," she stated emphatically and she quickly changed the subject. They made arrangements for the second week in January when her father would bring his bride to New York to meet Vanessa before returning to Cleveland. She hung up the telephone with mixed feelings: happiness for her father, a twinge of envy for his new-found life, and a dollop of self pity. She slept dreamlessly.

"Vanessa, I *have* to talk to you. May I come in?" Richard Bauman's face, shiny with nervous perspiration, poked in the door of her office.

"Of course. What's the matter, Richard? What can I do to help you?" She examined the worry lines on his forehead and the tense set of his body as he came in and stealthily closed the door behind him. She tried not to laugh at his gestures—it was so ludicrous to see the owner of the business slinking around like a thief in the night, not to mention that the walls of her office were entirely made of glass and anyone who happened to glance their way could see everything that went on inside.

"It's Power, that bastard. He's not here and it's nearly lunchtime already. I don't know what to do."

"He probably slept late—half the pressmen are still home asleep, even though your eyes mistakenly tell you they're in the next room. It's only their bodies that are here—their heads are really home in bed nursing hangovers from the Christmas party."

"You think it's funny, but it isn't. The men may be hungover, but at least they're here. *They* know how important it is to get the prints done now. We have to have Power here to proof and he isn't here."

"So call him, Richard. Tell him how vital it is that he get here right away. He has a contract with you, doesn't he? Don't be so afraid of him, Richard, he's not going to bite you."

"I am *not* afraid," he said defensively, effectively admitting that he *was* afraid, desperately afraid, although Vanessa did not know of what. Yes, Jacques was intimidating, but he was not so fear inspiring as to make Richard actually tremble before her eyes.

Bauman took a small box from his shirt pocket, opened it, and extracted a tiny green and black capsule which he popped into his mouth and swallowed with some difficulty, there not being any water with which to wash it down.

"Tranquilizers, Richard? Since when?" she asked him with concern.

"Ah, it's nothing, Vanessa. You know how harried I get at the end of the year." He dismissed the tranquilizer with a wave of his hand.

She looked more closely at him. Everyone at the atelier was usually fairly strung out the last two weeks of the year, Vanessa no exception. This fortnight was the busiest of the past fifty-two weeks, by far. It was the nature of the business to have to tie up all the loose ends by December 31 for tax purposes. The I.R.S. was extremely strict with companies involved in the art tax shelter industry and had been known to schedule spot inspections as early as the first business day of the new year to make certain all lithographs said to be printed in a certain year were, in fact, completed by midnight on New Year's Eve. Jacques Power's contract with Columbia Atelier was one such tax shelter.

But Richard Bauman exuded a terror Vanessa had never before seen in him. His hair, thinning to the point of baldness on top, had definitely turned whiter in the past few months. Funny, she hadn't paid close attention to Richard in a long while. He was—well, he was just there. Someone she saw daily, greeted, said good night to at five or six o'clock, and never thought of again until the next workday. Two deep furrows had sprung up seemingly overnight between his eyes, which now were clouded with worry. And two additional deep creases ran from the sides of his nose to the outward corners of his mouth.

"Richard, I'm worried about you. Call Power first and then I'd like to have a talk with you. I think you're pushing yourself too hard."

"I've called him. As soon as he heard my voice, he hung up on me. I don't understand—everything was going all right up to this point."

"And I'm certain it still is," she soothed. "There must be some misunderstanding. Call him back. Here." She picked up the receiver and handed it to him, noting the tremor in his hand as he took the black object from her.

She waited silently while Bauman held the telephone mutely to his ear for the longest time. "What is it?" she asked when he wordlessly slammed the receiver back in its cradle.

"Answering machine. 'Unable to come to the phone at this moment,' et cetera. I hate those damn things! Makes me want to say 'Mr. Bauman's machine greets Mr. Power's machine. Beep-beep.'" He tried to laugh, but the noise that came out of his mouth was more like a bark. Vanessa had a horrifying premonition that Bauman was going to break out in tears. She tried to think of something fast to comfort him. His emotions were overwhelming him, he wasn't thinking straight, that much was obvious to her.

"Richard, what's the worst? How much more work

has to be done? What I'm saying is, you must have *some* leeway to finish before the thirty-first."

"None."

"None? Not even a day?"

"None. He has to proof his prints now. Vanessa, will you go over to his studio and see what's going on. Please?"

"Me? Richard, I—I have a lot of work to do myself. I couldn't possibly—"

"Please, as a favor to me. It's so important, you have no idea. I know *you* could talk him into coming in, into finishing up the proofing."

"I'd rather proof the prints myself. I can do it twice as fast as Power can anyway." Although both she and Bauman knew what she said was true, her real reason was a desire to avoid confronting Jacques again, most especially in his own studio. She'd been enormously relieved that morning when she realized he wasn't at the atelier. Enormously relieved and yet quite disappointed as well. What *did* she want? She really didn't know.

"I couldn't let you do that," he answered quickly. He had the grace to look embarrassed, but he continued on anyway. "It's one of the terms of the contract that he do his own work."

"I see. Well, that's too bad," she said, her tone unmistakably hurt. She shuffled the mylars on her desk, a clear gesture of dismissal that she hoped Bauman was not too far gone to notice. But he seemed oblivious of her subtle intimation.

"It's nothing personal, you know. He has nothing against *you*, Vanessa," Bauman said quickly, anxious to smooth her feathers.

"No, not against me personally, I know," she said, although she wasn't certain she believed him. "Against *all* women, more than likely. Perhaps against the whole human race, who knows?"

"You're being unfair to him. I happen to know he's a very kind and generous man." Richard was the second person to speak of Jacques that way in as many days—perhaps there was something to the very divergent opinion Richard and her father seemed to have of Jacques. But when Vanessa looked at Bauman suffering an anxiety for which Jacques was responsible and still defending the thoughtless artist, she thought to herself that *Richard* actually was the kind and generous man—too bad his wife didn't see the good in him. Sadly Celia read the gentle part of Richard's nature as a weakness to be exploited to the fullest.

"I know all about Power and his charities, Richard. I find the image of Jacques Power as secret philanthropist hard to buy, believe me. But since the information came from an unimpeachable source and since you seem to confirm what I heard...all right, I'll go." She gave in with a sigh. "I don't want to and I'm doing it for you and you alone. Not because I think Power is such a nice guy—personally I think he's a real bastard. Does that word smear the ladylike image of me that you all seem to have around here?" But Richard hadn't even heard her swear.

"Oh, I love you, Vanessa. You're the greatest!" She winced. He lowered his voice. "You won't tell anyone, will you?" The relief that washed over Richard's face was so obvious she turned her face away, not caring to embarrass her employer by witnessing his raw emotions.

Ten minutes later she sat in a SoHo-bound taxi. The noon news blared from the radio. Vanessa's light blue eyes stared out the car's grimy window, oblivious of the raw and nervous tones of a radio announcer as he verbally painted the portrait of a bellicose world on the eve of the annual holiday that sanctimoniously celebrated peace among men—an ambush in the Mid East, kidnappings in Italy, guerrilla revolution in Central America. In a high-pitched voice that gave equal emphasis to Bronx tenement fires and global political unrest, the announcer intoned the weather report, predicting heavy snow for the Tri-State area tapering to flurries in the morning.

"Would you turn off the radio, please?" she asked the driver. "I can't stand all this peace on earth." He complied quickly, snapping off the news and immediately beginning to hum a rock tune instead. Her stomach churned with apprehension at the thought of seeing Jacques again so soon—and on his own turf. She had hoped to avoid him entirely, expecting that, as had happened in the past, his path and hers would have no reason to cross at the atelier. What if that woman was still in the loft when she arrived? She twisted in discomfort on the seat when she thought of how close she had come to sleeping with him. How close to being the great artist's latest one-nighter.

"... can't get any closer, lady. There's an electric company truck closing off the block. That'll be four fifty." The driver brought the taxi to a stop on the northwest corner of Jacques's street.

"This is fine, I'll walk." Vanessa paid the man, tipping him generously because it was Christmas Eve, then she walked up the block toward the now familiar entrance.

To her amazement, her feet carried her up the street, although at every step her mind urged her to turn and run. No matter that Richard Bauman seemed hell-bent on dragging Jacques to the atelier against his will. No matter that Jacques supposedly was generous to a fault. If he was, he hid it well, she thought bitterly. Certainly his treatment of her the night before had shown Vanessa precious little of his famous compassion for her feelings or her dignity. She had already convinced herself that Jacques's failure to appear at the atelier that morning had nothing to do with his near-seduction of her the night before. Near-seduction—whom was she kidding? It had been full surrender just lacking consummation! But not coming in to proof his prints that morning—that was a surprise. Didn't he know how vital his presence was? Was he unaware that every man in the shop was on duty today just awaiting his go-ahead? With nothing else on the agenda the entire crew would be paid for an idle day. If anything, Jacques was known as a professional. He might be moody and as temperamental as a boil, but the word in art circles was that he did as he promised—he was no prima donna. Surely a man of the world such as Maynard had described Jacques to be, a man who had been around, would not fail to meet a business obligation simply because a woman had turned him down. Or would he? Was he so accustomed to getting his own way that he refused to tolerate one rejection? Even angry as she was, she found that explanation for his absence hard to swallow.

A heavy, wet snow fell slowly, spotting her black wool coat and the hoods of automobiles that lined both sides of the narrow street, dusting the usually drab neighborhood into a softer landscape. In the vestibule she found his name on one of four brass plates and rang twice. To her surprise, he buzzed her in immediately without even asking her name. As she rode the poky elevator to the fourth floor where his rambling studio lay, her hands iced with apprehension and her stomach aflutter with nervous butterflies, she appreciated the sharp contrasts in the SoHo neighborhood. The bleakest industrial brick facade could and did secretly hide wildly luxurious co-operative apartments and spacious artists' studios in a city where square footage was possibly the most expensive in the world. Her musings were confirmed when the elevator door unexpectedly opened on the second floor and she was privileged to catch a quick glimpse of a converted loft through ts open door. Apparently each story contained just one apartment or studio and this one looked as if it were awaiting the arrival of a photographer from *Architectural Digest*.

When at last the elevator shuddered to a stop at the fourth floor she found herself looking directly at the strongly chiseled features of Jacques Power's face. His tall and lanky frame leaned casually against the wide-open door to his studio. He wore his usual costume of paint-smeared jeans and a blue work shirt, bleached by age to a soft white. The thin, faded cotton stretched tautly over his wide shoulders and his imposingly masculine form filled the doorway. Their eyes met and she saw in their hazel depths a tension that glittered palpably. There was a tightness in his limbs that belied the casual set of his long legs and the ease with which he'd folded his strong arms across his chest. He reminded her of a wiry cat poised to attack its unsuspecting prey.

"What are *you* doing here?" he asked rudely. A look of sheer annoyance descended over his freckled features, erasing the gleam of hopeful expectation she had first discovered in his greenish eyes. "Even if you *have* changed your mind, I can't see you now."

"Changed my mind! You conceited bastard, I'm here on business—remember business? The way we all earn our daily bread? Please don't think I've failed to notice that *you* live in the stratosphere," she enunciated clearly, sarcasm dripping from every word. "But the rest of us, the lowly peons, we put in workday after workday just for our paychecks." Of course, he'd assume she'd come because she'd changed her mind about sleeping with him—why hadn't she thought of that before she agreed to come here? "You've got a contract with us, Power. We're waiting for you at the atelier. The whole crew is standing around on one foot waiting for you to come in and proof. Or don't you care? *We* need the money, even if you don't," she said pointedly.

"Look, I've got other things on my mind, lady. I'll be in tomorrow." Lady! He'd called her lady like an angry stranger on the street. A stab of quick pain followed by an anger, unfamiliar in its quick intensity, shot through her.

"Tomorrow is Christmas. We need you *today*. Bauman is beside himself with worry. Why won't you answer the phone? What's your problem, Power? Are you mad because you didn't score last night? Is that what's troubling you?" Vanessa studied the lines of his face, but the strong light from the studio behind him made it nearly impossible to read his features. She brushed past him, forcing her way into the loft, much as he had done the first night at her apartment.

"I didn't ask you in. I can't see you, I tell you." He grasped her roughly by the wrist and checked her forward movement. "You'll have to leave!" Despite the thick wool coat and the leather gloves she wore, her head reeled as the familiar shock of his physical touch shot up her arm. Mingled with the heat generated by his hand the hot anger increased, threatening to bubble over. She forced herself to control the unaccustomed emotions he ignited in her. She had good reason to be here, she had promised Bauman. Knowing how vital Jacques's contract was to Richard, she repeated silently that she mustn't allow her own feelings to color her reactions to Jacques. Almost a hopeless task, she knew, but she'd try.

"This is strictly business," she repeated. "No matter about last night."

"I think last night *does* matter," he said. "But this isn't the time I want to discuss your neuroses."

"*My* neuroses! What the hell are *you* talking about, Power? My neuroses! You're the one—"

"I'm the one who read your signals correctly. You wanted me and I was prepared to deliver. What happened to you? I can't be expected to read the mind of some crazy old maid who changes her mind in the middle—"

"Crazy old maid! Deliver! You were prepared to *deliver* the goods like some prize-winning stallion on a breeding farm? I'm not so hard up that I need favors from *you* or any other man. You really are the most arrogant of men and I've met some *true* weirdos in my business."

"Listen, Vanessa, calm down. I told you, I don't want to talk about it now. Some other time, perhaps," he said coldly, attempting again to dismiss her.

"I never intend to discuss it again. I have no desire to see you or talk to you about anything after yesterday." The lie was difficult for her to say. What she really wanted was to pull an explanation from him, was to put her arms around his muscular body and start afresh, as if she had never seen Ruby here in the studio. She longed to believe any peacemaking words he chose to dangle for her approval and acceptance. Instead she laid her free hand on his other arm and said in a gentle and conciliatory voice, "Jacques, let's forget our past differences. Let's forget yesterday, please? Right now I need to know what I should tell Richard Bauman. He sent me here to see you. When we get this business straightened out, I won't bother you again about anything, I promise. Just tell me what you plan to do."

He looked as if she had slapped him. "That's fine with me, lady. Tell Bauman I'll come in when I'm good and ready."

"Jacques, this isn't because of—of you and me, is it? Because, if so, it isn't fair to Richard. He's a good man and he shouldn't be made to suffer because of what did—or didn't—happen between you and me. We can work things out, I know. In the meantime, he needs you."

"And he sent *you* to get me, right? Why you?"

"He couldn't get you on the phone."

"But why *you*? Why not come himself?" His voice was no longer cruel and angry, but she detected a weariness, a note of resignation that she hadn't heard before.

"I don't know, he trusts me, I suppose. Will you come? It won't take you that long. The printers need you now; they can't go on to the next step without your consent."

"I can't do it, Vanessa. I'd like to. I'm not in the habit of bailing out, but right now, I *have* to stay here. I'm waiting for someone. I simply can't leave."

"And it's more important than the entire atelier at a standstill, waiting for you? I'm sorry, I just don't believe you."

Jacques was silent. Conflicting emotions played across his face in the shadowless north light that came through the frosted skylights far above his head. A firm, stubborn set to his mouth told her he wouldn't say another word. Yet in a moment, with a quick intake of breath, he announced, "Look, I'm waiting for my mother."

"Your *mother*," she repeated with disbelief. "You're waiting for your mother?" She was missing something, she knew, but what had caused the finality of his pronouncement was beyond her comprehension. "I don't understand. Couldn't you see your mother later, after you proof the prints?"

"I haven't seen my mother in thirty-five years."

Now that the admission was out, an excitement danced in his hazel eyes. No wonder he had been so nervous when she arrived. Now she understood the wounding look of disappointment that had crossed his face when Vanessa emerged from the elevator.

"Your *mother*?" she said again. "How fantastic! In thirty-five years? But that means you haven't seen her since you were a little boy! Oh, Jacques, I'm so happy for you." And she *was* thrilled to hear his unexpected news, the flash of anger she'd felt before now mercurially gone. She hugged him spontaneously, then stepped back embarrassed at her unplanned gesture. Merely being so close to him, even for a moment, dizzied her. But he reached for her and wrapped his arms around her, squeezing her until she thought she'd faint.

"Actually I'm glad you're here. I've been dying to tell someone." He grinned infectiously and she found herself smiling back at his happiness.

"How did you find her after all this time?" she asked him.

"I didn't. She found *me*, I don't know how."

"You don't know how! You! Jacques, you're *famous*, remember? It'd be a cinch to find you. Besides, how many people have a French first name and an Irish last name like yours? You have to agree, it's a pretty rare combination."

"Well, I guess you're right," he replied, with a diffident flush. "She's French, you see. You've met my old man. You must have noticed there's little of *him* in me—so there must be a lot of her. At least I've always assumed so."

"Why did she leave, then?" Vanessa clapped her hand to her mouth as if to stuff the offending words back in. "Oh, Jacques, I'm sorry. That's none of my business and I shouldn't have asked."

"No, it's all right." Having told her his secret, Jacques was a new person, all his former coldness gone as suddenly as a quick August rainstorm. His eyes had been sparkling with excitement, but they clouded with a painful curtain of memory when next he spoke.

"She left Patrick, my father, not me. He wouldn't let her have me, so she had to go alone. It was agonizing for her. I think she left him because he's a bum, because he has an empty soul. I just know she couldn't stand the pain of living with an animal like my old man. Hell, you've seen him—all he cares about is where the next drink is coming from, when the next horse is running. I would have left him too, but I was only a kid and a kid takes what he's dealt in the shuffle as far as parents go. When you're small, you don't know the difference—your own parents are the only standards you have. When you get older you begin to realize that other kids get encouragement, their fathers don't call them pansies simply because they like to draw pictures. Other kids can count on their folks to be there when they need them. You see that and you begin to make plans to get out. But I don't think you'd understand what I'm talking about."

"You're right, I guess I had the kind of parents you mentioned, the other kind," Vanessa answered. "But I know what it's like to be abandoned." She stared at his wonderful face in amazement. How could she not have found him handsome before? Why had she been so fearfully intimidated by him? He was so warm, so anxious to be loved. His eyes danced and a happy flush lay on his freckled cheeks. What he had just told her unwittingly revealed worlds about his behavior, explained his coldness, explained his need to do everything for himself and to take nothing from others. She wanted to give him the love and encouragement he had always lacked. She longed to wrap her arms around his hard body and protect him from the pain of the world. She was as elated by his newfound joy as if the discovery of his lost mother were her own long-cherished dream.

"I think I could learn to love a man such as this one, this Jacques Power," she said to herself and was struck speechless when she saw an answering flicker of surprise in his eyes. Her own words echoed heavily in the suddenly silent room and she told herself that it wasn't possible she had actually spoken out loud.

"What? What did you say?" Jacques moved toward her. Vanessa fell back a step in confusion. Had she really voiced the words? Oh God, his eyes told her he had heard the spoken thought that lay like a weight between them in the still loft.

"You don't *have* to leave, you know," he said softly with an intensity that stripped her soul bare before him.

"Yes.... I must go. I—I didn't mean to say that. I don't know what came over me. Your mother will be here soon and I know you'll want to be alone with her." She backed toward the door.

"Vanessa, wait!" he called out, but she had wrenched open the heavy door and she fled blindly into the dim hall. When she reached the elevator, she turned back to him.

"Vanessa, please come back," he shouted again.

A doorbell rang behind him, three short, impatient bursts of the buzzer. He turned his head toward the sound. Painful indecision played across his rugged face and with a muttered curse he chose to respond to the imperious summons of the bell. The door to the elevator, still at the fourth floor, opened at her trembling touch and Vanessa ran into the protective car, her ears ringing in agonized embarrassment, the memory of his strong body pulled in two directions vivid in her mind. She knew she must leave, leave him alone to meet his mother. There would be enough time later for her and Jacques. She had seen the answering emotion in his eyes and the clear, new certainty of his look had told her all she needed to know for now. Her body tingled with sexual awareness, the touch and smell of him vibrantly alive on her arms. Oh yes! She could learn to love this man. She shivered as she suddenly *knew*, knew as intimately as her own familiar name, that she was prepared to admit that she loved him already. And what's more, *he* had wanted to hear the magic words she said. She closed her eyes and saw again the look of surprised pleasure on his face. She pressed her fevered head against a wall of the slowly descending elevator and wondered at the resilience of the human heart. She who'd been so certain she would never love again—who had not *dared* to love again—had just felt the unfolding of her heart—not slowly like the delicate petals of a perfect summer rose, but in an explosion of thirsty joy, like the first crocus of spring bursting through the snow to kiss the tentative shimmers of sunlight that announced the rebirth of life.

In a happy daze she went out of the building into the snowy street, not even irritated by the stout, impatient woman who bumped her rudely when she pushed her way into the creaking elevator even before Vanessa had left its dingy confines. Suddenly she understood why lovers sang of walking on air. She walked toward the corner to find a taxi, as buoyant as a lost balloon sailing above Central Park on a spring day, as free as a cloud on the horizon behind the Palisades. Even the air on the grimy SoHo street smelled of flowers. She had seen the birth of new flickers of caring in Jacques's expressive eyes, she knew she had. There had been no mistaking his look of pleased surprise.

Chapter Six

On the corner Vanessa gaily waved to flag down a passing taxi. Truly, a heavy perfume hung in the winter air. She even recognized the distinctive fragrance: Evening in Paris—that was it! That was the fluted blue bottle on display in the five-and-ten so long ago. The woman, the woman in the elevator! The same blowzy woman she'd seen before on this very street. Vanessa refused to believe what her senses screamed—that cow she'd passed simply *couldn't* be the woman Jacques happily awaited above. But who else could she be? A stab of cold fear pierced her stomach, exploding her elation. When Jacques saw the ruddy, swollen face, the strident circles of rouge.... When he saw in those narrow eyes a lifetime of raw self-indulgence....

Vanessa turned and ran back into the building, oblivious of ankle-deep puddles of black water that soaked through her leather boots. Savagely she punched the button to summon the elevator, punched it over and over until her ears told her the ancient car was approaching the first floor. The ride to four seemed interminable in the close car, its air heavy with the cloying scent of Evening in Paris. She fought an urge to gag.

Even before the elevator stopped she heard Jacques's voice raised in anger. The door to the studio stood ajar and she approached it on tiptoe, but the two people within the loft would not have heard the arrival of the fire department. She stopped outside and narrowed herself against the wall of the corridor.

"Get your hand off me and get out of here or I'll call the police, I swear! I never want to see you again, do you hear?" Jacques thundered.

The woman answered him in wheedling tones. Her back must have been to the door. Vanessa couldn't make out her whining reply.

"All you *did* for me!" he shouted. "*What* did you do for me?" A sudden tiredness filled his words and his voice cracked. "You walked out on me. You just up and left—left me alone with Patrick. I can see now that I was better off alone with him. At least he stayed with his kid! Now you want money because I have it and you don't! Why should I give you anything? I'm not going to, you know, no matter what you say. It's too late for you. Why did you leave me?" Anguish echoed in his words, the cry of a small boy abandoned years before.

"All right, if that's how you feel," a martyred voice responded with resignation. "You were a rotten kid in the old days and I can see nothin's changed since then." The woman had turned toward the door; her words were as clear as they were wounding, tearing through Vanessa like a scalpel opening flesh. "You and Pat—the two of you always wantin' something from me, always hangin' on my skirts, noses runnin'. I was too young to be tied down, livin' in that shabby place. No money, no nice things never. I needed to have *fun*. I wanted to be *free*. I couldn't stand the two of you no more."

"Get out! Get out of here and don't ever come back!" Jacques's shout reverberated through the loft and out the door to the dim corridor where Vanessa cowered against the wall holding her breath. The sharp staccato of high heels clicked toward her from the direction of the loft's entrance. She tried to make herself invisible. She did not move: Where was there to hide anyway? She kept her eyes lowered, unwilling to look on the face of the woman who claimed to be Jacques's mother. She saw the scuffed white toes as the patent leather boots raced past; she smelled the overpowering stench of cheap perfume hanging in the air in the wake of the woman's ample figure.

When the elevator clanked shut she expelled her breath unevenly in the sudden silence and approached the entrance of the loft. Jacques stood ready to shut the door, one hand tensed on the jamb. The hollow-eyed look on his face congealed her blood. It was a cold, angry, latently violent stillness. His lips were white with rage.

"Jacques, let me talk to you!" She extended an arm toward him.

"No! Get out!"

His voice boomed out, slashing through the tense air like a whip. He hurled the heavy door toward her with all the force behind his sinewy arms.

Vanessa flung her body toward Jacques before he was able to slam the door shut in her face.

"You *have* to let me in! I must talk to you." She leaned against the door. He pushed to close it from the other side. His force was much greater and she knew she was losing the battle. With a last ounce of reserve strength she gave a mighty shove and the door yielded a scant inch.

"Jacques," she begged. "Let me in—only for one minute."

"I really don't want to see you now. Just go away and leave me alone." His deep voice was hollow with the painful effort of speech.

She searched her brain for something to say that would make him open the door and admit her. She longed to comfort him. She already knew how the hard, unyielding muscles of his rigid shoulders would feel on the soft arms she would offer him. Through the small crack in the door she looked at him with blue eyes unconsciously wide and appealing. For what seemed a long moment neither of them spoke, although she knew mere seconds had passed. *I don't know what to say to prove I don't want to hurt you*, she implored him silently.

Perhaps he heard the words her mind formed because he opened the door at last and walked quickly back into the studio without a word. She stared at the hard set of his wide back as he strode across the gigantic room and perched himself on a single stool that sat in front of a messy drawing board under one skylight. He folded his arms over his chest and stared at her, as if to say "Show me!"

She approached the stool. There was no place for her to sit. He had effectively isolated himself.

"What do you want now?" He finally broke the all but unbearable silence.

"I heard what happened," she answered.

"Everything?"

"Enough," she admitted in a quiet voice. "I don't know what to say. I'm—I'm terribly sorry, Jacques." She took one step toward him. He shoved the stool back against the drawing board with a boot-clad foot. The scrape of its wooden legs echoed mournfully in the cavernous room. Vanessa stopped and waited for him to speak.

"The bitch! Oh, hell, it doesn't make any difference," he said with an obvious effort to speak casually. He looked away and she could see his throat working above the open collar of his blue shirt when he swallowed hard. For a moment she thought he would cry and her heart tore in two just to witness his pain. She took another tentative step toward the drawing board.

Jacques turned his back on her like a wounded animal, and leaning his elbows on the tilted drawing board, he buried his face in his hands.

"Why don't you run along, Vanessa? I'm not up to visitors right now." His rough workman's hands, so unlike her preconceived idea of an artist's sensitive hands, muffled the stab at lightness in his words.

She examined the way his wild red hair curled over his collar. His neck was so strong. The muscles of his back stretched the washed out cotton of his shirt across the lines of his shoulders until she wondered that the soft fabric did not tear. She could tolerate her empty arms no longer. She longed to touch him. She allowed her damp coat to slide to a heap on the floor and she approached the forbidding lines of his back, slipping her arms around his neck and gathering his tense body to the yielding softness of her breasts.

"I'm not a visitor, Jacques. I don't want to run along." Did she dare? She felt poised to plunge on the dangerous edge of an abyss whose sides were too sheer to climb out of once she ventured to jump. "I want to stay with you. I—I love you, Jacques."

God, she'd said them. She'd said the oft-read, oft-heard words so exceedingly difficult for her to actually form and utter to another human being. At last she had pronounced the long-alien syllables and they sounded perfectly right on her lips. She had believed she would never use those three small words again, but as soon as she made up her mind to say them, they simply slipped from her tongue like liquid silver, confirming a truth that had become the very fiber of her body, but to which she had just now given a name. When had that miracle happened to her? She felt the tension of his muscles ease imperceptibly under her gentle touch. She sighed with relief, a long warm sigh that ruffled the curls of his hair.

He said nothing. Vanessa didn't care. She did not seek an answer. Just the fact that she had told him how she felt was enough for her. All she wanted now was to offer him a small measure of comfort in *his* agony. Later, later there would be plenty of time for him to learn that he loved her too. She knew he would love her. She had never been so sure of anything in her life. A quick flame of certainty danced in her heart.

His rough, freckled hand came up and covered hers where it rested on his chest. She smiled with contentment.

Now all that was left was to get Jacques's mind off the horrible confrontation he had just been through with the woman who claimed to be his mother. Of course, she *was* his mother, Vanessa did not doubt the fact; there was even a slight but unmistakable physical resemblance. Yet Vanessa was incapable of relating the raw and obscene vermin she'd just seen to this suffering man she loved. The woman may have given birth to Jacques, but in no way had she given him life. No correlation was remotely possible between her and the sensitive and gifted artist whose heart beat quickly beneath the pressure of Vanessa's comforting hand on his broad chest. Perhaps if she could convince Jacques to accompany her back to the atelier, he would concentrate on the prints, put off thinking about that woman and her incredible demand for money after a lifetime of neglect. Then later, when the pain had dulled a bit, when he felt capable of replaying today's shocking revelation with more distance, perhaps then he might find the ability to see the woman's disgraceful arrival in a new perspective.

"Jacques, get your coat and come with me," she urged him in a soothing tone.

Jacques cleared his throat before he raised his head to respond. "Where? Where do you want me to go with you?" His voice had nearly returned to normal.

"Come back with me to the atelier. You can work on the prints and get your mind off what just happened for a while. It'll be good for you, darling."

In the moment of silence that followed her words an atmosphere charged with electric discord exchanged with the placid air of the studio.

Jacques jumped to his feet, upsetting the wooden stool, which toppled to the floor with a crash. In one quick sweep of a muscular arm he scattered a neat pile of sketches for his next painting from the drawing table. The paper fluttered noiselessly to the floor.

"Darling, is it? Darling!" He turned to face her, his eyes filled with scorn, his face white with rage.

Vanessa threw her hands up in panic to protect herself. He seemed coiled to deliver a blow.

"What is it? What did I say wrong?" she screamed. She backed up blindly, actually afraid Jacques would hit her with his fist. The blood drained from her own face when she looked through her fingers into green eyes crazed with anger. A nerve at one temple pulsated with his fury and she saw the blue veins pounding under his fair skin.

"What's the matter, are you scared I'll hit you? No matter how little you think of me, beating women isn't one of my hobbies. *You* go back to the atelier and proof the damn prints! *You* do it, *you're* the frustrated artist, aren't you? I for one don't care how they come out. Go back to Bauman and tell him you got the goods delivered, you got the precious job done— that's all you want from me anyway. Everybody wants something! You're no better than that tramp who was just here wanting to be my mother all of a sudden after a lifetime. No, you're worse! At least she laid it on the line—all she wanted was money off the top, no involvement. Well, I have to admire her honesty, which is a quality they neglected to cultivate in you in that fancy prep school you went to. 'Jacques, I love you. Jacques, when can we go to bed together?' You make me sick! You turn my stomach! Get out of here and *stay* out!''

He grabbed her coat and purse from the floor and savagely wrenched her by the arm. He spun her around and propelled her toward the door to the corridor. Enraged, he shoved her into the hall, throwing her coat after her. The door slammed with an explosion. Pieces of plaster trickled to the floor behind the wall.

Her heart had stopped. She'd been incapable of uttering a single word during his tirade. She stood mutely in the hall and forgot to breathe.

She ran back to the door and pounded on it with the heel of her fist.

"Wait! You've got it all wrong! Open this door right now! Jacques, open up, let me in. Let me talk to you!"

There was total silence behind the blank door.

Finally the tears came and filled her eyes, spilling over to course down her pale cheeks. She struggled to fill her lungs with air. She sobbed in misery. She scooped up her coat and purse and ran to the stairwell, racing noisily down the steep metal steps, in a panic to quit the building before anyone heard the hysterical sobs coming unbidden from the depths of her breast. She ran out onto the now gray and ugly street and thanked the gods above that an empty taxi waited at a stoplight on the corner.

"I checked with Power and you were right, he wants you to proof for him," said Richard Bauman. "So get to it, Vanessa."

"Yes, Richard."

"Of course the men will have to stay overtime to get the first series pulled, but if you work fast, it'll just be a few hours. It's too bad, being Christmas Eve and all."

"Yes, Richard."

Dully she turned to leave his quiet office. Incredibly, he hadn't noticed her haggard eyes, red-rimmed from crying. How could he have missed the funereal look on her face? She felt like someone had just pulled her out of a coffin and forced her to act the role of a normal human in a normal world ignoring the evidence that she was already dead. But no one had looked at her twice. Not even Maynard whom she'd passed in the hall on her way to report to Bauman. Of course Bauman was concerned with the contract— nothing else could penetrate his nervous mind. And Maynard was leaving work early, transported with pre-occupied ecstasy at the thought that he and Antonio would be spending the Christmas holidays in Vermont as guests of a famous women's clothes designer at the Coty Award winner's mammoth alpine ski chalet in the mountains.

"And when you're finished, come back and have a holiday drink with me. We owe ourselves a little celebration for pulling this one out of the hat, eh, Vanessa?"

"Right, Richard."

She returned to the press room and proofed methodically. The job was simple, really. Jacques's work was impeccable and barely needed correction. She took solace at her own ability to do the job mechanically, without need for thought. And a measure of comfort that just enough technical involvement was necessary to keep her mind off the unthinkable accusations he had hurled at her.

Every so often she would tremble and feel a pervasive cold in her limbs. And tears would roll unheeded down her cheeks. Once Vinnie, the foreman, put his burly arm around her and asked, "What's the matter, kid, missing your old man at Christmas?" His dark brown eyes were soft with compassion.

"Like the devil, Vinnie. I feel like an empty house just waiting for my man to come home." Why not? Let him believe she was thinking about Andrew. She rubbed her cheeks with the back of her closed fists so as not to smear her face with fresh ink from the press.

How easy it would be to hate Jacques after what he had called her. But she did not hate him, she loved Jacques—it was that simple. And she didn't care how he had abused and insulted her; he had been deeply wounded only moments before he screamed those hateful epithets. He'd been torn apart by the discovery of his mother's true character and he'd lashed out at the closest human being. God, it hurt to think of the ugly, accusing words he had shouted at her, but Vanessa was glad she had been present to witness the agonizing drama unfold. She understood Jacques better now, oh, so much better. She had never considered herself the cheerful, optimistic type; she was more pragmatic and realistic. Her imagination never soared; she worked doggedly for what she sought. Perhaps those very qualities had kept her from her planned career as an artist. And how neatly he'd used the knife of *that* knowledge on her! But now she felt that some good would come of the horrible scene that afternoon. She would have another chance with Jacques. She would *create* another chance with him. Make it happen, force him to listen to her. Teach him, if necessary, how to love her.

Maynard threaded his way toward the press where she proofed the prints Vinnie was pulling. Despite her heartache, she had to smile at his costume. She turned her head away so no one would see the amused grin she was unable to keep off her lips. Lucky Maynard, the only person who could get a few vacation days before December 31. Bauman liked to explain that the curator's duties were not as essential as other jobs, but Vanessa had overheard one or two of Maynard's screaming temper tantrums to which Bauman readily capitulated. Today Maynard wore knickers, patterned argyle knee socks, and a two-colored Icelandic sweater across the front of which a red reindeer cavorted. If he had been just slightly overweight the outfit would have looked ludicrous. How unlike him to show up in the office dressed like this; usually he came to work in clothes that made him look like a distinguished older model who had stepped from the pages of a men's fashion magazine.

But Vanessa had seen Maynard's closets and she knew he had a costume for every activity.

"Already dressed for the slopes, Maynard? Couldn't you find any *lederhosen*?" She giggled despite an effort to keep a straight face.

"Oh, I found them easily enough, but I've already had my fun with them. They no longer give me the thrill they used to. I've lent them to Antonio and he looks smashing in them! He has great legs, my sweet." He looked down at his knee socks as if to decide if his own legs were already over the hill.

"I hadn't noticed. I'll have to look," she answered.

"Knock off for a minute and come into my office. You look like you could use a little rest." He eyed her pale face and red-rimmed eyes. "I have a little Christmas gift for you and then I'm leaving for the mountains right away. It's already snowing like the devil. We thought we'd get an early start."

"Hence the knickers?"

"Be prepared, et cetera," he responded with a twinkle.

She ran back to her own desk and found the small box she had tucked away in a drawer for him. She followed his path into the climate-controlled curator's archives where wide, deep drawers of catalogued prints lined every wall. A ten-foot square desk dominated the center of the room. On every inch of the desk samples of Jacques's new prints were spread flat, fresh ink glistening under the lights.

Maynard and she opened their gifts at the same time, since he was eager to leave the office as soon as possible to beat the crush of holiday traffic.

"We'll have our usual Christmas dinner when I come back. I feel as if I'm deserting you, dear, but how could I turn down this coveted invitation?"

"You couldn't! Don't be silly. I'll be all right, you know. I have to start being alone on Christmas sometime, Maynard."

"I pray this is the last year you will ever be, Vanessa. Oooh! I love this little enamel! How precious, how perfect! Look at the adorable little violets!"

"And this book, Maynard. *Sonnets from the Portuguese.* How beautiful! I will always cherish it." She kissed his lean cheek and he kissed her hand.

"It's a first edition," said Bauman, entering the office. "He showed it to me the day he found it." He admired their gifts politely, obviously impatient for them to finish the pleasantries.

"I'm getting right back to work, Richard. I just wanted to say good-bye to Maynard."

"No, forget it. We're packing it in for the day."

"We're nowhere near finished, Richard. You won't make the deadline. What happened?" Her hands caressed the soft florentine leather of the book of poetry. She had to do something with them since they were trembling again. She feared what Richard was about to say. A haggard look around his mouth told her there was trouble brewing.

"*He* wants final say-so now. Power called—no more printing without his go-ahead. God, why did I ever sign him up anyway? Someone has to take him the proofs so we can do the finals first thing the day after Christmas."

"Okay, so what's the problem?" asked Maynard.

"Nothing that can't be solved. You'll take him the prints, won't you, Vanessa?" he asked sweetly.

"Me? Oh, no Richard. I've done enough for one day. Find someone else. I—I don't think I'd be the best"—she chose her words carefully—"the most effective person for the errand." Twin thrills of excitement and fear coursed through her veins. She longed to see Jacques, longed to tell him he was wrong, totally wrong in his accusaions of her. What would she say when she saw him? How would she make him see the truth? He had been blindly angry, absolutely beside himself with rage. She understood. He reminded her of a dog who had been beaten so often by cruel owners that he could no longer trust people. He must be very scarred. She would love him; she would show him that someone could be trusted and that she was that someone. She knew in her heart that if she had another chance to be with him, to talk to him, to touch him, Jacques would understand at last.

Maynard was eyeing her. She felt his eyes expectantly on her although she had turned to face Bauman. They were both awaiting her reply. It wouldn't do to appear too anxious or Maynard would worry about her all during his holiday. He was like a mother hen at times, imbued with a curious and often misdirected maternal instinct thrust on him by the genetic gods. He had already warned her quite clearly that Jacques Power was not to be trusted in affairs of the heart. Without even a glance in his direction she sensed his strict disapproval. What could she say now to demonstrate to Maynard that she was reluctant, while at the same time imply to Richard that she was willing to go to Jacques whenever he wanted? She searched vainly for the right words.

Richard took her hesitation for refusal.

"I'm your boss and I *order* you to go," announced Richard with uncharacteristic bravado.

She heard Maynard's quick intake of breath as he moved into her line of vision. They exchanged a mute glance of shock and Maynard rolled his eyes up to the ceiling. A large electric clock hummed behind them on the wall of the quiet room. Outside the presses had gone still.

"If you *don't* go, I'll lose the atelier," said Bauman in the sudden quiet. "You'll all be out of a job, every one of you here." He hesitated to swallow a lump in his throat. "I'm asking you specifically, Vanessa, because while it's true you already know Power, more because this is Christmas Eve and, God forgive me for taking advantage of you, but you don't have a family to go home to after work tonight. I feel terrible— I'm out on such a limb that I'm using my best friends and I'm desperate." He began to cry.

For a moment Vanessa and Maynard were stunned into an embarrassed silence. Then she crossed swiftly to Richard's side.

"Richard, I'll go. Of course I'll go. How could you doubt me?" She laid a hand on his arm. "I'll do whatever you need. I always would, Richard, you know that. Please don't cry."

Her blue eyes spoke to Maynard silently and clearly over Bauman's lowered head. *You see, I have no choice,* they said triumphantly. ❦

Maynard gave her the high sign behind Bauman's back and he slipped out the door without a word, waving goodbye as he went. The red reindeer on his chest heaved a sigh of relief.

"There's only one small problem, my girl."

"What's that?" she asked warily.

"Power has gone to his place in Connecticut for the holiday."

"Oh, Richard! What are you getting me into?" She didn't try to hide the elation in her voice.

Vanessa raced home to change her clothes. Before she was able to leave the city with the precious proofs wrapped in brown paper at her side in a rented Oldsmobile, a stormy darkness had fallen. Traffic, snarled anyway due to the holiday, snail crawled in the quickly accumulating snow. She drove with tense concentration through the clogged arteries that led to the New England Thruway. Eighteen-wheeler trucks flung slush over the windshield and she worried she'd miss the sign to Weston, but at last she turned north, following the handwritten directions and crude map Bauman had provided.

The highway to Weston was much worse, heavily choked with snow. She drove in ruts left by slow-moving cars ahead of her on a winding country road. Finally she turned off on a narrow lane, which, according to the map, led to Jacques's house. Her cold hands cramped with apprehension. The headlights of the Oldsmobile scarcely illuminated the edges of the wooded lane. The car skidded and bucked against the drifts that were rapidly clogging the private right-of-way.

At last she saw a lone light burning at the end of the road. She nudged the Olds as close to the house as possible, hoping the wheels were still on the driveway and not on the lawn. There was no way to tell where the car was in the blinding snow.

As there had been no other house on the lane, this one had to belong to Jacques. Struggling with the large package in the wind, she made her way to the main entrance. From the sound of running water she heard to the right and the distinctive shadow of a wheel in the darkness, the house seemed to be an ancient converted mill. She lifted a heavy brass knocker and let it fall, listening to its echoed thud. After a long moment she knocked again. No answer. A cold stab of panic pierced her. Hadn't Bauman called? What was wrong? Wasn't Jacques here?

She knocked once more, this time as loudly as she could. She couldn't stand out here all night! Refusing to contemplate a return drive to the city, she tried the heavy door. It swung open easily.

"Jacques! Are you there? Anyone home?" Silence. She stood at the open door and listened. She called again. Directly inside the front door hung a massive canvas, unmistakably a Jacques Power. She shut the door and propped the unwieldy package against the wall.

"Jacques, it's Vanessa VanderPoel. Are you here?"

From the hall she saw a fire burning in a large stone fireplace in the next room. She followed its flickering light through a high-ceilinged, dark room and extended her hands to the welcome warmth of its flames, allowing her down coat to fall open in grateful acceptance. Someone had to be home. No one would leave such a roaring fire unattended. Yet all the lights in the room were extinguished. Could he have gone out for a moment? On a night like this?

She called again. Without waiting for an answer, she turned on a lamp at the side of a large sofa in front of the fireplace.

"Ye gods, you scared me!" Jacques long legs lay extended on the sofa. "Why didn't you answer when I knocked?" Her heart was thudding rapidly, as much from the shock of seeing him so soon as from finding him a bare three feet away.

"What the hell are you doing here?" he growled.

"That's some Merry Christmas. Look, I just drove all the way from New York—it took me more than three hours and I'm tired. There's really no need to be so incredibly gruff with me. Let's try to be nice to each other. Didn't Bauman call you?" If he hadn't called....

"I'm not answering the phone. Turn off the light."

She glanced at a half-full bottle of Armagnac on the table. He looked as if he had been drinking the brandy since afternoon and hadn't noticed that darkness had fallen. She turned off the light as he had asked. "Mind if I have a drink? I'm really tense from the drive. The roads are awful."

"Help yourself."

"Shall I drink it from the bottle?" she asked him sweetly. But if she had expected him to prepare her a drink, she was mistaken.

"Glasses in the kitchen," he mumbled, indicating a dark doorway to the right of the fireplace.

She found the kitchen and the lightswitch. The cozy room pleased her. Lots of Dutch tile and copper, a rough country hutch, skylights—now covered with snow. She selected a brandy glass from the hutch. She switched on the radio and heard that the New England Thruway had been closed due to the storm. On hungry impulse, she went to the copper refrigerator, opening the double doors and peering inside. A tray of cold cuts and cheese lay prepared on a shelf. She found plates, napkins, and two forks. Balancing her glass, she returned to the darkened living room. Jacques had not moved.

"Have you eaten? Let me fix you a plate of food." Silence. "Didn't you know I would be coming, Jacques?" *Don't you know how much I want to be here?*

"No."

"Well, I can't go back tonight. The roads are closed. They say it's going to snow all night." She was secretly pleased. He appeared unaffected by the news, but he didn't speak.

"Where can I sleep?"

"There's only one bedroom."

"I'll sleep here on the couch."

"Suit yourself."

She ate in silence. He merely picked at the food, pushing it away after a moment. He refilled his glass, topping hers off without a word. This was ridiculous, she thought. They could not spend Christmas Eve alone together in awkward, painful silence. She knew what troubled him, but was so afraid to mention his mother that her throat ached. And yet, the tense silence weighed heavily on her.

"Why are you alone here for Christmas? Where's your Christmas tree?"

"What do I need a Christmas tree for?" he grumbled.

"For the spirit, I guess."

"I suppose you have one in your apartment."

"Well...no."

"Why not—no spirit?" His voice was cynical, deprecating. "I assumed a girl like you would have all sorts of cute Christmas decorations—needlepoint stockings, mistletoe."

"Something wrong with that?"

"I guess not. I bet you still have the ornaments that hung on your tree when you were a baby."

"I do," she confirmed. "Does that bother you for some reason?" When he did not answer she asked him, "Where's your father? Is he at church?"

"Church! My father at church! That's really rich." He laughed bitterly.

"I thought he was in town to spend Christmas with you," she said, confused.

"He and Ruby went to Las Vegas to do some gambling. That's his Christmas present to himself. From me, I guess you could say. Although against my will. No, not really against my will. I don't know what I mean. What the hell do I care what he does with the money?"

So it was Ruby and Mr. Power. Of course! Those two together made so much more sense than Jacques and Ruby. She smiled in the darkness. "What does he do? For a living, I mean."

"He doesn't do anything. He's retired from the

docks. Although I don't remember when he actually *did* anything. Sometimes he'd work, sometimes not— they got laid off a lot. And there were plenty of Mondays he didn't go in even if a job *was* waiting. It's nothing new to have Patrick disappear at Christmas. Nothing new at all."

He no longer sounded bitter. Instead a note of resigned sadness had crept into his low voice. He seemed to be remembering Christmases from long ago years. A somber tint colored his green eyes. Her heart went out to him, a small boy seemingly alone in the world—on Christmas morning, the culminating day of a child's fantasy life. She felt her own eyes fill slowly with tears as in her mind she pictured the lonely scene.

"And what did *you* do? When your father wasn't there on Christmas morning?"

"Do? I—I don't remember." But she saw the long-forgotten pain her words evoked. He looked away from her. After a lengthy silence she said, "Wouldn't you like to talk about her, Jacques? About your mother?"

"I don't have a mother," he snapped. "Never mention her to me again. Nor to anyone, do you hear?" He covered his face with his hands.

"I haven't," she answered simply. "I never would."

He gave her a long and searching look, which she was unable to read in the dim light. At last he said, "No, I know you wouldn't. You would never do anything like that. Just instinctively you would know." His throat was tight and his voice caught on the last word. "I'm sorry, you shouldn't have to be burdened with my problems. It's just, well, it's just as if—"

"As if she had died today." Vanessa finished the sentence for him.

He looked up in surprise, a new appraisal of her written in his haunted eyes. "How do you know that?"

"I'm no stranger to the pain of death. My mother died when I was ten and my husband is dead. You learn to live with the pain. It never goes away, but it does get easier as time goes by. Not much easier. I guess it's like a habit or like the color of your eyes or your skin. It becomes a part of your fiber."

"I'm sorry. I didn't know. I never knew you had been married. I thought you were one of those liberated career women who chose to be single. I've said some pretty rotten things to you, haven't I?"

"Forget it. How would you have known?" She watched him bury his head in his hands once more. Her arms ached to comfort him, but the fear of another cruel rejection held her back. One moment he seemed so open to her. The next he might lash out in anger and pain. She recalled vividly the emotional scene in his studio. And yet, he looked so vulnerable, so small as he hunched mere inches from where she sat in the flickering firelight.

She reached out and laid a hand on his arm. The familiar tingle snaked up her nerves.

"Jacques, go to bed. Sleep. It will be easier tomorrow." She stood and pulled at him. He came up from the couch and stumbled against her. She wrapped her arms around his waist and held him tightly. "You need to sleep. Come to bed." He allowed her to lead him to the bedroom, which lay behind the fireplace se

and which shared the warmth it provided. She pulled a quilt from the bed and turned down the sheets.

"Take your clothes off. Get into bed." Then Jacques began to undress, exposing as he did so the muscles of his shoulders, the incurving line of his spine. The lower half of his body lay in the flickering shadows of the now-dying fire. When he had removed all but his shorts, he threw himself on the bed, lying on his side, curling into himself in pain. Vanessa crossed silently to where he lay, seemingly asleep already. She drank in the sight of his wiry limbs. She lifted the edges of the soft quilt and pulled it up to cover him, smoothing it over his shoulders.

Chapter Seven

Vanessa returned to the living room and picked up the remains of the cold supper. In the kitchen she washed up, checked the weather report once more, and turned out the lights. She did not need the radio to tell her how heavily the snow was falling; the strange silence of snow was all about the house. She threw two stout logs on the fire and returned to the bedroom where Jacques lay. He had not moved. She crossed to a window and stood for a long moment watching the snow swirl against the black windowpane.

Slowly she pulled her dress over her head and leaned forward to ease it off. She removed her stockings. At length she slid into the bed next to him. Her arms sought the fuller body at her side and she wrapped them tightly around his rigid shoulders. He opened his eyes and looked deeply into hers. He was like a wild animal, his eyes haggard, his tousled hair falling over his forehead. Her own eyes implored him silently. She took his head and laid it on her breast. He allowed her to lull him. She listened to the crackling of the logs in the blanket of snow silence.

"My husband died three years ago today," she whispered. She felt Jacques try to lift his head. "No, don't move. Just rest." Rhythmically she caressed the hair at the back of his neck. "More than anything in the world I wanted someone to hold me, to tell me that everything was going to be all right. That *I* was not going to die. That I was going to live. I don't think we should make love—I just want to hold you. Can you understand? I need to hold you. Do you want me here?" She thought she felt him nod his head, an almost imperceptible movement. She silently pleaded with him, pleaded with love for him. After a while, out of sheer exhaustion, he slept.

Convinced by the measured pattern of his breathing that he was sleeping, she began to cry softly. She wept for the sudden dissolution of Jacques's childhood dreams. For the shattering impact of the powerful despair that had stolen Andrew from himself and from her. For her inability to give Andrew the comfort she prayed Jacques was now drawing from her arms. She tightened her grip on his wiry body and drew him even closer to the fullness of her breast. When the flow of tears ceased, she lay dissolved by a maternal desire to protect Jacques from any more of the pain she had known so intimately. She felt an urge to open, to receive, to enfold his helplessness in her strength.

The quilt was too warm. She must have dozed near morning, she didn't know when or for how long. She lay sleep-drugged and unreal. But all during the long night her limbs had tingled with acute awareness of the touch of his muscular body next to her in the bed,

to every movement of his legs, to every rustle of the
sheets, to every changed nuance in the pattern of his
breathing.

And then she felt a soft hand on her breast, very
soft, caressing her skin so lightly she had to awaken to
make sure she had been touched. She opened her
eyes to see that Jacques was bending over her, his
head propped on one hand, his elbow resting on the
pillow next to her head. His mouth was half open, his
hazel eyes were tender, with such an expression of
unfamiliar gentleness that she did not move.

"Only a touch of you," he said.

She held her breath in the stillness. She had never
felt anything like the warmth of his hand gently caressing the smooth skin above the lace of her slip.
Tentatively his long fingers slipped down to the valley
between her breasts. She felt herself dissolve within,
grow warm and soft. He bent his head and touched his
mouth to hers, lightly brushing her lips. A tender kiss,
reminiscent of the first meeting of their lips—it
seemed so long ago now. He held his mouth on hers
gently, without pressure, until her own responded.
Only then did he touch the tip of her tongue with his.
His hand was moving, exploring her exposed skin,
following the contour of her breasts. She thought that
if she closed her eyes he would not stop. And she
wanted him to go on, wanted his gentle fingers to
touch her everywhere, to explore in all her secret
places. The warm languor grew, grew and spread
throughout her vibrating body. She inhaled the rich
aroma of him, the tangy citrus scent that seemed to be
a part of him, an evocative odor that owed no debt to

soap or to cologne. She inhaled the rich scent of sleep that hung over them both. Slowly he pulled away the sheet and quilt. She knew his eyes caressed her languidly; she felt them on her skin, on the full curves of her breasts. His free hand touched one shoulder, then the other and he gently lowered the straps of her slip, exposing her breasts to his gaze. The fire in the hearth had died in the night and cool air caressed her nipples, making them stand erect. His mouth closed over one breast, the warmth of his tongue impelling it to even greater hardness. She drew in her breath unevenly. He kissed her mouth again. They kept their lips together, the tongues meeting for an interminable moment.

Now his scent was like a forest of precious woods—aromatic cedar, eastern sandalwood. Lying with eyes closed at his side she felt transported on a carpet of desire and fantasy. She did not dare to open her eyes. If she looked, Jacques would be gone. He would arise and leave, depriving her of his touches and caresses. She lay as if in a trance, allowing his long fingers to undress her. Adeptly he raised the slip above her head, handling it as if it were of the finest silk. She felt him leave the bed, knew by the rustle that he was removing his shorts, his back to her. Still she lay as if hypnotized. She felt as if she were falling into darkness, into an abyss of unknown desire, a desire so shaking, so overwhelming, that it blotted out all fear of him. He fell toward her and covered her with quick kisses. She felt his breath on her, on her eyelids, on her neck, her throat. She was made senseless, each kiss like a gulp of wine, adding to the warmth that seeped through her limbs. His body warmed her body, each inch of them pressed together. She knew that if she kept her eyes closed he would take her. By now his hand was lightly stroking the soft skin of her thighs and feeling in her the trembling quivers of pleasure, the delicious sensations each gentle touch ignited. His mouth grew more and more avid, responding to the answering hunger of her limbs. She turned to him, grasping his hard body to hers, ravenous for the taste of him.

In an instant they ceased to be two bodies. Breathless murmurs of need and passion united them in mutual desire, flooding them with wave after wave of urgent demand.

They lay tangled in the sheets, enfolded in the scent of love that hung heavily in the air. Vanessa saw for the first time that the storm had stopped during the night. A brilliant sunlight flooded the room, warming the ocher tiles of the floor, its strength intensified by the reflection from the snow. Dust motes danced in silly abandon, borne by the shaft of sun that penetrated the casement windows. She turned her head slowly to look at Jacques. He seemed to be asleep. She studied the face behind his habitual mask, the vulnerable curve of his cheek, the sweet half-smile of satisfaction on his wide lips. The gentle and loving face of a trusting boy, she realized. She sighed with contentment and drifted into a half-sleep of her own, unmindful of the weight of his body on her arm.

When next she awoke, it was to the smell of bacon burning. The bed was empty at her side and the fire had been rekindled in the hearth. She jumped from the bed and found a silk robe in the bathroom. Quickly washing her face and combing her hair, she followed the telltale haze of smoke into the kitchen.

"Merry Christmas, Vanessa!" He was at her side, his long arms thrown around her, hugging her as if he wished to crush her ribs. A light of happiness glinted in his eyes, which appeared to be the green of jade in the sunlight streaming through the skylights. She looked up. He followed her gaze.

"I've already been up there and shoveled off the roof. We need the light. Hurry up, get dressed. We have to go out and cut a tree. What's Christmas without a tree?" She giggled in happiness at his transformation.

"I have nothing to wear!" she resisted.

"Oh, just like a woman," he hooted. He left the kitchen by a door she had not noticed before and returned in a moment with corduroy pants and a pair of boots. "These should fit. Hurry up. Breakfast is a disaster, but I think there's some cereal and milk around."

"I'll cook something," she offered.

"No, later. Let's find a tree first." He was so filled with enthusiasm, like a child on Christmas morning unable to choose between his gifts from Santa Claus, she had to laugh. He walked quickly to the bedroom and yanked open the door of an antique pine armoire, pulling out shirts and sweaters and throwing them on the bed.

"Choose something. It's cold—take two sweaters. Here, this is warm. Or this one." He chose a fisherman's knit, rejected it, chose another.

"Jacques, slow down. Give me a chance. I would like to take a shower. I'm hungry too. Hold on!"

"God, I feel wonderful!" He crossed to her and grasped her by both hands, pulling her around in a circle. " *You're* wonderful. Beautiful. Warm and soft. I'd like to draw you. I'd like to paint you. Watercolors. Soft and hazy. You're a fantastic woman!"

She looked at him in amazement. Was he the same Jacques Power she had known before? His spirits were bouyant beyond belief.

"Are you always like this after making love?" she asked him, a twinkle in her eye.

"I don't know. I don't think so. There was something fantastic about this morning. The texture of your skin, the smell of you. Don't you feel it? Don't you feel different? Alive?" he asked eagerly.

"Yes," she confessed after a moment. She did not add that she no longer remembered the last time she had made love. It was long before Andrew had died, she knew. But even searching back in her memory, she could not recall ever having experienced the transporting ecstasy she and Jacques had shared that morning. She admitted to herself in wonder that until today she had been sexually unfulfilled and that she hadn't even known it. "Yes!" she shouted, infected by his wild enthusiasm. "Yes, I feel terrific! And I'm going to take a shower." She broke free of his arms and went into the bathroom.

She washed her hair and soaped herself all over, humming tunelessly, forgetting all her hesitations about Jacques and his reputation. Forgetting the agony of her past obsession with him. Forgetting too the cruelty he had shown her in his loft. All that had passed between them before today detached from her consciousness and floated down the drain like so much soapy water. She was, for the moment, a woman who gave everything to the experience—without inhibition or fear. She bathed herself in the sheer joy of being with him on Christmas morning.

The corduroy slacks were too short, but they fit her. She vowed she would not ask to whom they belonged. All that was part of the past. The boots fit her as well. She chose one of Jacques's sweaters, a periwinkle-blue wool that matched her eyes this morning, and combed her wet hair, noting in the mirror a vibrant new sparkle in her eyes. She decided to wear no makeup, not even a touch of lipstick on her mouth, which was rosy and swollen from his kisses. At last she joined him in the kitchen. He had found a coffee cake and a package of frozen sausage, which they ate with relish after Vanessa fried the meat on a restaurant-sized stove.

"What a fabulous stove! Do you cook a lot?" she asked him.

"I can't cook at all. Just learning to press a few buttons on a microwave oven was hard enough," he answered between mouthfuls. "The stove was already here when I bought the place. And what interested me was the solitude, the woods, and the privacy. I'm thinking of living here full-time. I've started construction on a studio. I'll show you after breakfast."

"So this great kitchen just goes to waste? Too bad."

"Not exactly. There's an Oriental couple who lives here. They take care of the house for me. She's a good cook and I'm up here almost every weekend. So the stove gets plenty of use. They're off for the holiday, but they'll be back late today. Do you know how to cook?''

"Well, I *can* cook. That's not exactly true. I'm ... I *used* to be a pretty fair cook, but since I've been living alone, I don't do much cooking. It's hardly worth the effort for one person. Although they say you shouldn't live that way when you are widowed. You should indulge yourself a little, live as if you're important." She wondered if he would remember what she had told him the night before.

"Who's 'they'?" he asked her, smiling.

"Oh, you know, the experts."

"That's a bunch of rot! There *are* no experts in living. We all go around the track just once. I do what I want to and everything works out all right. Don't you think you're important?"

"Sure I do. And I know *you* do."

"What does that mean?" he asked quickly.

"Nothing, I guess."

"How did your husband die?" he asked her suddenly.

She hesitated too long before she answered. "An automobile accident."

"You don't sound convinced. Were you with him?"

"No, I wasn't with him and yes, I'm convinced he died in a car crash. He's really dead. It's only that I think he crashed his car purposely, killing himself." She hesitated again and when next she spoke her voice was low with wonder. "Why am I telling you all this? I've never told another soul!"

"That's all right." He laid his hand over hers on the pine table. "We don't have to talk about him if you don't care to. Sorry I asked."

How unlike Jacques to apologize, she thought. "I don't mind," she said quickly. And she realized that she *didn't* mind talking about Andrew with him. She told Jacques of the long and deepening depression that had culminated in Andrew's untimely death. Later she was to think back on the quiet and attentive look on his face and she was to remember the solicitous interest he had shown in the story of a young woman left abandoned and bewildered by an illness over which she had no control. She was to wonder just what had gone through Jacques's mind as he listened to her speak of those painful months now so far away in the distant past. Had he planned all along to take advantage of her candor? But that was later. That morning she shared the story of her pain with him in an effort to explain herself to him, she supposed. And she was not unmindful that her story might serve to take his mind away from the encounter he had endured with his mother the day before.

And Jacques did seem to forget the horror of the previous day. They left the dirty breakfast dishes in the sink and ran out into the new-fallen snow. Frolicking like children, they threw themselves down its knee-deep softness and made angels with their arms. They found a small tree growing two hundred feet behind the house in the woods and Vanessa watched as Jacques hacked it down with three sharp blows of the ax he had brought with him from the barn. They erected the tree outside on a deck reached through

French windows off the living room. Jacques found
two strands of blinking white lights in the barn and
they arranged them carefully on the branches of the
sweet-smelling pine. When Vanessa stepped back to
admire their work, Jacques came up behind her and
enfolded her in his arms. Kissing her neck, he
whispered in her ear, "I don't know when I've ever
been so happy."

And Vanessa had sighed with her own happiness.
She was unaccustomed to the feeling of simple contentment—like a trip to a foreign country unvisited
for a decade—strange, changed, but nevertheless
slightly familiar.

Later they sat on the couch in front of the cavernous fireplace and she listened wordlessly as he, at last,
spoke of his mother. His feet were crossed on the
rough table in front of the couch. One arm was
around her shoulders. Both their cheeks were rosy
from the cold outside followed by the sudden warmth
of the crackling fire. She felt at total ease in his presence, as if they had been dear friends for all their
lives. His eyes were far away as he told her about his
childhood after his mother had left their home. He
told her as if he were reading from a printed page,
detaching himself from the events.

"I really don't remember her. I really didn't, I
mean. I must have been about four years old, perhaps
five—I'm not certain. All I know is that I was too
young to read and one morning I woke up and went
into the kitchen, expecting her to be there. When she
wasn't, I went into their bedroom. The room smelled
of her—she always wore a strong perfume and she

seemed very feminine and soft to me. She had blond hair, lots of blond hair, which she wore down around her shoulders. I thought she was very beautiful with her blond hair. My red hair comes from my father's side of the family. He's Irish and she was French—that's where I got the name Jacques. But I guess she really isn't French, I don't know. She doesn't have a French accent—perhaps she's French Canadian? I could ask my father, I suppose. We never talked about her after she left, but everytime anyone mentioned the French he'd be so angry he would nearly have a stroke, so I always assumed that she was French.

"She wasn't there and neither was my father. He was at work, I guess. As I said, I couldn't read yet, but I saw she had written words on the mirror above the dresser in lipstick. Big red letters, not a long message." He stopped talking for a moment.

"Well, I knew she was gone, I don't know how I knew it, but I did. They'd had a terrible fight the night before. I don't know what they fought about because I always covered my ears with pillows when they fought. They fought all the time, so it wasn't because of the fight, that I knew. And she often left me alone, so that wasn't it, either. But I knew and I was really scared. I thought he had left too, you see. I thought they fought because of me, because they didn't want me, and that they were both gone.

"Eventually my old man came home from work. I heard him coming up the stairs, those heavy boots he always wore. We lived on the top floor. And I could hear he was alone, that she wasn't with him. I remem-

ber how I felt as if it were yesterday. I was so relieved
to hear someone coming. I was hungry and tired. I'd
probably been crying all day. And I was scared. I
knew he'd blame me and probaply beat the tar out of
me. I was so scared I wasn't able to move when he
came in the kitchen door, just stood there glued to the
floor and still in my pajamas. When he saw me there I
said, 'Mama's gone' and he said, 'That whore, good
riddance.' I didn't know what the word meant, but I
was afraid to ask him. He never mentioned her again.
We never mentioned her name again, not once.''

Jacques got up and stoked the fire. He threw
another thick log into the flames. He returned to the
couch and sat again at her side. He sat hunched forward with elbows on knees and cracked his knuckles
absently.

"As I grew older I realized what a jerk my old man
was. He drank too much, had a terrible temper, was
lazy and uncouth. In short, a man with no visible re-
deeming features. Somewhere in me was growing a
need to express myself artistically. At first I thought I
wanted to be a musician, to play the piano. But we
couldn't afford a piano—we never even had a telephone until I was in my teens. Paper was cheap, so I
started to draw, fighting him every step of the way. He
thought I was really queer and he used to say things
like 'You never got any of that namby-pamby stuff
from *my* side of the family.' Naturally I assumed the
differences between him and me came from *her*. I
used to fantasize that she was some kind of French
aristocrat, so sensitive and esthetic and lovely that she
couldn't bear the pain of living with a brute like *him*

any longer and that's why she left. But you know why she left—you heard her say so yesterday."

"Yes, I heard her," said Vanessa.

"So now, it's a new ball game." He laughed a short, harsh laugh.

"Well, Jacques, you said it yourself, there are no experts. But I must say it reminds me of stories I have heard of people—adults, not children—who find out late in life that they're adopted. It shakes them to the core, but it also explains to them why they've felt all along that something was amiss."

He searched her eyes for some forbidden reaction and smiled in pleasure when he did not find it there.

"Were you expecting my pity?" she asked him. "No, I don't pity you. My heart breaks for the four-year-old boy. But for you, the man, I have nothing but unqualified admiration. You survived, you *more* than survived—you made the best of all that happened and rose to unexpected success by sheer talent and ambition. And you will now, I'm certain. You'll get on with your life and put this long chapter to rest. And I hope you won't allow it to make you into a bitter person." *Any more than you already are,* a tiny internal voice added silently.

"I'd like to make love with you," he stated.

"Here?"

"Right here. Why not? What's to stop us?"

"Nothing. Yes, I'd like that." She pulled the blue sweater over her head. She watched his long fingers unbutton the shirt she wore. She stood while he removed her clothing and then she opened the buttons of his shirt and removed his. They lay on the couch.

Vanessa gave herself over to the erotic sensations that grew increasingly warm as Jacques gently ran his hands over the curves of her responsive body. He began to kiss her tenderly, first her lips, then her neck and each breast. The urgency that had marked their first attempt at lovemaking was gone, replaced by a comfort and languor that allowed her to feel no impatience. She felt only the growing pleasure of expectancy. She lay passive, thereby increasing the state of all her sensibilities.

Jacques followed each curve of her lovingly, seeking to take possession of her body with his hands. His lips followed his hands, searching out the secret pleasure centers of her being. He seemed to know where next she wanted his kisses to fall, what hidden part of her demanded to be warmed by his tender mouth. She lay pliant in his muscular arms, hazy in the anticipation of each caress. Her skin glistened everywhere from his kisses. She watched her own hands as if detached when her fingers entwined themselves in the curls of his wild red hair, trembled as his avid mouth showered her body with scores of kisses. When he parted her legs and gave his attention to the silky skin of her inner thighs, she pulled his head to her with a soft moan. Her quickened fires told him the moment he discovered the center of her ardor. He lingered in his want for her, delaying his own pleasure, but savoring the erotic anticipation he derived from providing Vanessa with ecstasies she had never before imagined to exist between a man and a woman. She wished for him to never stop. She wished for him to keep her forever poised on the keen, thin edge of this strange new abyss of delirium. But before too much time had passed, just as she became acutely aware that she could bear his fervent kisses no longer, he offered his mouth to hers and they abandoned themselves freely to each other, two lovers melting together in the exquisitely postponed joy of unity.

"You know I have to go home soon, my sweet," she whispered in his ear, fearful of calling him darling.

"Must you? I don't want you to leave. Stay the night, Vanessa." She loved the way he said her name, hesitating as no one else did between the *n* and the *e*. He lay alongside her, his gentle hands, which looked so rough, smoothing the silky skin of her hips.

"I have to be at work in the morning for the final run of your prints. You'll be there, won't you? Do you want to drive in with me tonight? You could stay with me if you like." She did not want to go too fast, but after all, he'd invited her to stay another night with him.

"No, my car is here. I'll have to drive it in anyway. Please stay, you can get an early start. The roads won't be too crowded the day after Christmas."

She sighed. "I'd love to, but I have to be there before eight thirty, before the printers come in. I would have to go to my apartment to change clothes first. That means I'd have to leave here before five! Why don't I simply wait for you to go over the proofs now so you won't have to come in at all tomorrow if you don't care to. That means you won't have to go to the atelier until it's time to sign the prints, Jacques."

"Sign the proofs?"

"No, sign the prints. You don't have to do anything except look over the proofs I brought up for you to okay before the final run. Don't you remember?" The air in the room felt suddenly cold despite a crackling fire in the fieldstone hearth. She shivered.

Jacques stiffened. "I think I hear the Changs coming in the back door," he said suddenly.

"I didn't hear anything," she said.

"You'd better get some clothes on. I'll get Chang to shovel out your car so you can go home."

He jumped up from the couch and headed into the bedroom. Vanessa scampered after him, but he was in the bathroom with the door closed and the shower running. She pulled her own clothes on quickly and ran a comb through her hair, which refused to cooperate the way hair always did for the women in the books she'd read.

She went to the entrance hall in search of the package of proofs. When she returned, the bedroom was empty. She found Jacques in the kitchen, dressed to go outdoors.

"Guess I was wrong about Chang. I'll go out and shovel the driveway so you can leave," he said without meeting her eyes.

"Do you have another shovel? I'll help you."

"No, you're already dressed to go."

"It'll just take me a second to change."

"No, forget it."

"Is anything wrong?"

"No," he answered curtly.

"You seem different—changed somehow."

"It's all in your head," he said as he went out the back door, slamming it behind him.

She listened to the harsh, rhythmic scrape of the shovel through the leaded panes of the windows. What had happened? Suddenly he was cold and distant, much like the day she'd first met him in Bauman's office. Perhaps it was all happening too fast for Jacques. She was fearful of smothering him with the love that trembled within her simply bursting to be set free after so long. She would be more careful, more distant with him until he grew accustomed to her.

She glanced around the inviting bedroom, so unlike the business-only atmosphere of Jacques's SoHo studio. A warm curly pine corner cupboard held one side of the room, its soft wood glowing with the copper patina of age. Above the fireplace hung a muted primitive portrait of a pioneer woman holding a rosy child in her lap. Her face was both stern and serene, an earth-mother who had taken her harsh life seriously, no doubt. On the wide chestnut floorboards, also polished by the years to a burnished glow, a handwoven American Indian rug brought the only splash of vivid color to the subdued room. The quilt on the double bed might once have been garish, but it was a prized antique now and its soft pastels had lost their brilliance long ago.

This was the house to which Jacques came for rest and care; this was the haven where he retreated from the world. She admired his taste and his collector's eye. The boy genius of the abstract art world collected primitive Americana in the privacy of his own home.

Come to think of it, the only piece of his work she'd
seen here was the imposing oil painting in the entrance hall, the unmistakable Power that announced
that she'd found the correct house. She wagered few
people knew of this passion for homey antiques. She
wagered even fewer had actually been his guests in
this converted mill tucked back in the isolated woods
of Weston.

The grate of the shovel had stopped, resumed with
a different rhythm. She looked out the window. A
smaller man had taken Jacques's place at the heavy
task. The Changs must have returned. She sat and
leaned against the hard rungs of a Windsor chair near
the fireplace and waited for him to come back. She
wanted to see him alone, not with the Changs around.
She dozed.

A soft knock at the door brought her awake.

"Missy, the car is free. Mr. Power says you may go
now." An Oriental woman of indeterminate age inclined her head slightly and was gone as quietly as she
had come.

"Where *is* Mr. Power?" Vanessa called after her
retreating back.

The woman returned to the door of the bedroom.
"He's in the kitchen. You want coffee?"

"Yes, thank you. I'll join him there." Vanessa followed her to the kitchen. Jacques was at the long pine
table where she had shared breakfast with him so happily a few short hours before. He did not look up
when she entered. On the scarred pine before him
were a mug of coffee and an empty snifter of brandy.

"Want a drink?" he asked, refilling his glass.

"No thanks, I'm already sleepy. Guess I dozed off for a bit." Perhaps he had come in and seen her napping; perhaps he had not wanted to disturb her.

"Umm" was all he answered.

Mrs. Chang laid a mug of coffee on the table in front of Vanessa.

"Jacques, what's wrong? Have I done something to offend you? Please, please look at me."

He looked up then, but only to signal her with his eyes that she was not to speak of personal matters in front of Mrs. Chang. Other than the pointed message, their green depths were unreadable.

"Did you look over the prints?" she asked him nervously. "How did you like them?" Not in years had Vanessa sought approval for her work like a child standing below the desk of her teacher, one foot rubbing on the other in agonized suspense. She felt as if her entire future depended on the whim of his reply.

He had reviewed them. He had one or two suggestions for the yellow plate, but in general he was pleased with her work. She let out a sigh of relief, surprised at how tense she had become. Her unpolished thumbnail had been digging a tiny line into the distressed pine of the table as if she wanted to wear a new groove on its ancient surface, wanted to mark somehow one of Jacques's possessions, some tangible property that those beautiful rough hands of his touched often in the course of an ordinary day.

When she finished the coffee, she rose and thanked Mrs. Chang, asking her where she bought the aromatic Jamaican blend she'd seen her grinding for a second—or was it third?—cup for Jacques. The Chinese woman was as effusive as her employer had been terse, urging Vanessa to return soon, to drive safely, and to eat more vegetables. While the women talked, Vanessa felt Jacques's impatience take the form of a living specter behind her back in the warm and coffee-scented kitchen.

When she had put on her coat and boots, Jacques walked her to the rented Oldsmobile, his feet large and sure-footed, hers small and unsure on the leather soles of city boots squeaking in the new snow that sparkled under the outside lights like so many iridescent soapflakes.

She waited in the still snow while he placed the brown paper package of proofs on the passenger seat. Chang had warmed the car. Jacques opened the door on the driver's side for her and stood politely aside so that she could enter the car.

"I'd like to kiss you good-bye," she said finally, when he made no move to do so.

"Sure." He offered her his lips. She kissed the cold, firm skin lightly, torn apart inside by his lack of response. She inhaled the sandalwood scent he naturally exuded. She wanted to tell him how much she loved him, wanted to recapture just a glimmer of the intimacy they had shared during the special day. But she was afraid to scare him. She suspected he was incapable of handling the emotions she had identified earlier in his eyes. Now, to her sadness, she was unable to name the source of the change in him. He'd gone from flying euphoria to this steely cold tolerance of her presence, just verging on rudeness.

"I can wait, you know," she told him softly. In the house a phone was ringing.

If he wondered to what she referred, he was not saying. There was no answer. He slammed the door soundly. She drove down the narrow lane away from him.

Chapter Eight

Somehow Vanessa lived through the next day. Work helped, helped a lot. She threw herself into the task for all she was worth, as much to put the pain from her mind as to involve herself directly with a creation from Jacques's own hands. The prints were beautiful—absolutely stunning—and Bauman was beside himself with pleasure at their quality.

"We'll be finished in time, thanks to you, Vanessa. You did it, you got the business in on time. All that's left is for Power to come to sign and remarque and we'll make the deadline." He rubbed his hands together rapidly with glee.

"And when will that be, Richard?" She thought she was fairly successful in keeping her voice casual, but the inside of her mouth felt hot and oily as she spoke. Pain did funny things to the body.

"Oh, we have him down for day after tomorrow in the morning. That still gives us time in case something comes up and he has to postpone. You'll get a print, of course. What shall I tell him to write on it?"

"Why don't you leave it up to him? He may not want to give any away. Some artists don't, you know."

"No artist who ever printed in *my* atelier stiffed the chromist!" he sputtered with indignation.

"This one may be different, Richard. Power is... a...a maverick, I guess you could say."

"What an imagination! You remind me of Celia, always looking for the negative in people."

"I don't think I'm like that, am I?" She thought of herself as exactly the opposite, trusting to a fault. Maynard often teased her that she couldn't walk through Grand Central Station without emitting a siren call to the con men who hid in its bowels waiting for an innocent person on whom to lay a hard-luck story.

"No, of course you're not. You just seem cynical about Jacques Power, that's all. I admit he's been one of the more difficult artists we've ever dealt with, but—oh, Vanessa, it's been worth it!" He held up one of the lithographs, a study for "Hudson River." He smiled with jubilation. "This one will sell out overnight."

"I agree."

She missed Maynard. She wanted to confide in him, to solicit his advice. On the other hand, she was pleased he would be gone for a week. He had warned her about Jacques, called him a womanizer, an egocentric *artiste*. He had said the word with great scorn. She was embarrassed to confess that just what he predicted seemed to be happening to her: Her heart was tearing in two. If things had not worked out with Jacques by the time

Maynard came home from Vermont, she'd be able to handle herself better since enough time would have elapsed for her to feign a normal demeanor. And if Jacques called—well, there'd be nothing to hide. She was incapable of concealing her feelings from Maynard for long—*if* he was looking, that is. But right now Maynard was totally involved with Antonio and the decorator's glittering social world. She was safe from his perceptive eyes as long as *their* liaison was trouble-free.

Another day passed. She finished all her work, everything she had to do before the December thirty-first deadline. She went to Richard and volunteered to help out in the curator's office since they were short-handed while Maynard was away. Bauman accepted her offer happily, blissfully ignorant of the sadness of her mood. She was as nervous as a high-strung diva and had to bite her tongue more than once during the long hours she spent with the gum-cracking assistant curator. She couldn't understand how Maynard could tolerate the girl's slow-witted work. He'd often complained, of course, but now Vanessa had more compassion for the cross he had to bear daily. The girl was Celia's niece; she'd have this job until she ran off with the unemployed electric-guitar player she had been seeing behind her parents' back for three months. Vanessa heard all about him and even managed to eke out a not-too-mendacious compliment when asked to admire a grainy snapshot of his rock band. It helped that she couldn't quite distinguish the face behind the long hair.

On the way home from work Vanessa explored the

Portuguese block in the West Forties where almost
every shop sold discounted electronics. She purchased
a middle-of-the-line answering machine. The salesman demonstrated how to work the machine and
even helped her to make up a message, giving her tips
about how to word the recording to protect her privacy.

"I hate to get one of these machines on the line
when I call someone," she said as the clerk wrote up
the purchase on an American Express form, "but it's
sometimes important not to miss...um...business
calls."

"Yeah, you'll love it. Very convenient. Sign here."

By ten o'clock she went out to a pay phone on the
corner of Columbus and Seventy-second Street, next
to the all-night newstand, to call herself. She was certain that either the machine or her telephone was
broken. But when she returned, the red light indicating that a call had come in was on and she played back
the tape to listen, crestfallen, to her own hollow, tinny
voice as it came out of the speaker.

Two o'clock in the afternoon. She'd chosen the stool
facing the corridor to Bauman's office so that she
could see Jacques when he came into the atelier to
sign his completed prints. She worked through lunch,
covering for Shelly while the grateful girl extended
her short lunch hour to meet with her boyfriend at his
East Village walk-up. Vanessa's head bobbed up and
down all day, as scores of people traveled the busy
corridor, but no one had red hair, no one was tall and
strong and walked with the self-assured gait she'd

come to associate with his long, muscular legs. When she could stand it no longer, she went to Richard's office with a contrived question to which she already knew the answer.

He gave her a funny look, but a long and detailed answer. She nodded, she hoped appropriately, willing her eyes to convince him she was listening to his droning description. When he had finished, she said lightly, "Wasn't Power supposed to come in today to sign his prints?"

"Did Shelly forget to tell you? I'm sorry, I thought you knew—we shipped everything to his studio yesterday. He wanted to sign and remarque there, said it was too noisy here at the atelier with the presses going."

"It must have slipped her mind," she answered. "Who took the package to him?"

"He sent his own messenger."

She could bear the silence no longer. When she arrived home that night, she called him at his loft, but a disinterested voice from an answering service told her that he was out of town. She punched out the Connecticut digits with an ice-cold finger. Mrs. Chang answered effusively and told her in a singsong voice that Mr. Power was in town, he was *always* in town on weeknights. They did not expect him for the holiday nor until the following Friday. Vanessa thanked her, asked her to say that she had called, and hung up pensively. On impulse, she called the answering service again and left her name and numbers—home and work.

She attended a post-Christmas performance of *The Nutcracker* with Miss Weissman. When the night came she hadn't wanted to go, but they'd ordered the tickets months in advance and she felt too guilty to disappoint her neighbor. She'd even gone into the elderly woman's apartment with an excuse ready on her lips, but before she opened her mouth the pale, gentle lady had eyed her and said incisively, "You look a bit anemic, Vanessa. Man trouble, I'll wager. Is Douglas giving you a bad time? I can't understand why he hasn't proposed yet. Nothing that Tchaikovsky can't cure, is it?"

"Lena, Douglas is not my type. And if he is about to propose, I'll be the most surprised person on the West Side! I—I guess it's just that I miss Andrew a bit," she lied again. "I don't think I could sit through *Romeo and Juliet* tonight, but *The Nutcracker* is another story. If *that* can't cheer me up," she said, laughing, "I'm hopeless." Making a mild joke of her heartache cost her more energy than she thought she had.

So they supped early and lightly at La Crepe and then watched the adorably precocious children pirouette smartly before them on the stage. At intermission they ordered a sherry in the lobby and Vanessa, like any tourist, gaped at the Chagall paintings above their heads. Funny, she'd been to Lincoln Center perhaps a hundred times since she moved to New York. She'd seen and admired the Chagall murals—she'd studied art, after all, and art was her business. But she'd never *felt* their soaring life before. She stared in awe at the massive scale of the work. The sherry was exquisitely dry and wood-flavored on her tongue. All her senses were newly acute. Why not? She was in love: She knew it in every cell of her body. The only surprising thing was that strangers didn't come up to her on the street, despite the recently acquired, dusky circles under her light blue eyes, and say, "Excuse me, miss, I see you are in love. Can you tell me how it feels to love someone?"

"Vanessa, where are you? In outer space?"

Vanessa came awake and looked at the white halo of hair neatly finger-waved around Miss Weissman's birdlike head. She'd been to the neighbourhood hairdresser in preparation for their night out at the ballet.

"I'm sorry, Lena. You were saying? I must have been daydreaming."

"Oh, my dear, I was in love once. It is a transporting experience. I remember, though it all happened so long ago."

'You were? What happened to—to *him*?" She looked at Lena's familiar face with renewed interest and tried to imagine the wrinkled flesh taut again over the bones, the snowy hair black or brown and crackling with the life of youth.

"My family didn't approve, although I was no spring chicken at the time, and neither was he. A matter of background and religion—those things were quite important in my day. I—we—what does it matter now who? Neither of us had the courage to grab what we wanted. Too cautious, I suppose you'd say."

"And what happened to him? Did he marry someone else?"

"No, he never married. He's gone now. He died about five years ago. Alone, like me."

"Oh, Lena, I'm so sorry."

"Don't think about it again, my dear. We all have our regrets; that's mine." She replaced her empty sherry glass on the stone banister of the balcony overlooking the Lincoln Center lobby. "Shall we go back to our seats? The next act is about to begin. They rang the bell while you were communing with Chagall."

She thought about the empty core of Lena's life all during the ballet. When she returned to the apartment she checked the answering machine and saw that only Douglas had called in her absence. He was leaving for Europe.

New Year's Eve came. The atelier was utter chaos. Somehow they finished the work, the books, the day, the year. They always did. Every December was the same. If she chose to, she could look forward to a lifetime of them, she knew. At six o'clock she had a drink with Richard in his office to celebrate the successful conclusion of the year and to bring in the next, more placid year, they hoped in their toast. She drank the burning liquid out of a wrinkled paper cup from the water cooler and said good night. Richard and Celia were to leave the next day for Palm Springs for a week of much-needed rest.

She went to the movies alone.

Maynard returned, bringing her a can of Vermont maple syrup as a gift.

"Maynard, what will I do with a *gallon* of syrup?"

"Make pancakes and enjoy," he grinned, pleased that she was pleased with his extravagance.

"I haven't cooked a pancake in more than three years!" she objected.

"Well, what are you waiting for?"

She invited him and Antonio for brunch the following Sunday morning, rising early to prepare crepes, her fingers awkward at the long-forgotten task and her mind preoccupied that Maynard, a renowned gourmet cook, would find her inadequate.

When they had eaten and had drunk the bottle of cold Moet et Chandon that Antonio had thoughtfully provided, they sat back in a contentment and the men regaled her with "in" gossip of the antics of the famous designer's set as played out Christmas week in Vermont. She plucked a fresh strawberry from a basket of out-of-season fruit Maynard had somehow obtained in New York in January and watched their eyes as they glanced at each other fondly during the intricate stories.

"And how was your Christmas? What did you do?" Maynard asked her, at last.

"Miss Weissman and I went out to dinner," she lied. "And my father called from the Caribbean. He's getting or has already gotten married again."

"To whom? Do you know her?"

"No, he thinks I do, but I don't remember her. He's bringing her to New York next week to meet me."

They discussed what would be the appropriate wedding gift for such a union and decided to visit Cartier's on Monday afternoon, although Maynard was adamant that Tiffany's was the better store—a much greater selection.

Vanessa agreed with Antonio that while the departments in Cartier's were limited, the smallness of the store made the service better. She wondered how the two men could be so heated in their discussion and then drop the subject and go on to another as if no cross words had passed between them.

"I see Jacques Power has an opening this coming week," said Maynard. He eyed her closely.

"I didn't know. That gallery on Madison? I thought he already had a show on there." She forced herself to be off-handed and jumped up from the couch to offer more coffee all around.

"He's changed galleries. He must be a terror to deal with, what do you think, Vanessa?"

"It's not *his* fault, Maynard. That woman in the Madison Avenue gallery was a harpy! No wonder he wanted to change." She hadn't meant to be so shrill, so quick to defend Jacques. Maynard was certain to see through her. But he didn't seem to notice. She missed the silent look he and Antonio exchanged across the room. "Who's representing him now?"

"That young Middle Eastern woman," Antonio answered in his charming Dominican accent. "She has a new place in SoHo. We met her in Vermont."

"Didn't he tell you about it?" asked Maynard.

"Me? Why should he tell me anything? I haven't seen him since Christmas. Since *before* Christmas," she said with studied emphasis.

She gathered up the cups and saucers and took them to her small kitchen. She splashed cold water on the veins inside her wrists. She shouldn't drink champagne, especially in the afternoon, she told herself.

On Tuesday an invitation to the SoHo gallery's opening was delivered by messenger to her at the atelier. She marched immediately into Maynard's office to confront him with the accusation that he was meddling in her life. She hoped against hope that he would deny having anything to do with getting her the coveted invitation, silently praying that Jacques had put her name on the list.

"I merely thought you might care to attend, dear child," he said in a wounded tone. "I don't meddle in others' affairs."

"Others' *lives*, not affairs." She stamped out of the room, ignoring the gum-cracking Shelly.

She made plans to attend. She sent her most sophisticated black wool gabardine suit out to be pressed and she went to the Courrèges Boutique and purchased a silk blouse the color of Amantillado sherry, a blouse so frivolous, so magnificently sensual with its hundreds of tiny tucks and pleats that she was unable to stop stroking its silky folds where it lay on the bed in its tissue paper after she brought it home.

Douglas returned from Europe. Vanessa had hardly spoken with him since before Christmas, neglecting to return his sporadic messages on the answering machine and missing most of his between-trip calls to her at work. When he did get in touch with her finally, she wasn't up for their usual dinner in a restaurant and planned to say she was busy, but as a compromise, she decided that since the brunch for Maynard and Antonio had been so successful, she would invite him to a casual supper.

He came into the apartment wearing a gray three-piece suit and a red striped necktie. She was surprised at his formal dress, but then she realized he might have just come from work; she had never inquired into his daily schedule. As he came in she thought again that his quiet, serious manner was in contrast to his calling as a salesman, but Lena had told her repeatedly that Douglas made a "nice" income. Nice—that word again. *Nice* fit Douglas like a glove. His height, his sandy hair, his regular features, made him an acceptable escort. Nice.

Douglas removed his horn-rimmed glasses and polished them carefully. He pecked her on the cheek. "I have a serious matter to discuss with you, Vanessa."

"Come into the kitchen, then. I'm finishing up the crepes and I don't want anything to burn." As they passed the dining alcove she glanced at the table set for two. Nothing had been forgotten. China sparkled and sterling gleamed, but there were no candles. Although she did not believe Lena's prediction that Douglas was planning to propose, she had no intention of encouraging him by creating a romantic atmosphere. Before Jacques, she had been perfectly content to go out with Douglas, who demanded nothing from her, emotionally or otherwise, as she had asked nothing from him, certain that Douglas, the perennial bachelor, was satisfied with the status quo.

He had never implied in any way that Lena's suspicions were true.

Vanessa poured a cup of syrup into a small pan. She set it to one side of the stove on the Formica counter. Just before serving the crepes, she would warm the syrup.

"Take off your jacket and relax. What's on your mind?" Douglas removed his jacket and hung it carefully on the back of a chair at the dining room table. He kept his tie and vest on. He perched on a stool at the open end of the long, narrow kitchen.

He cleared his throat. "We've known each other a year, isn't that correct?"

"More or less," she agreed. She couldn't really remember when they had met.

"I think we know one another fairly well. You don't have any habits that I find objectionable and I am certain you could say the same about me." His tone implied that he had none, that the topic was beyond discussion.

"True," she answered warily.

"I am now thirty-five years old. I have an established career. You have had a decade to work and to see how you liked having a job."

Vanessa's hand, poised to turn a paper-thin crepe, stopped in midair. This was it, then. Lena had been right! Suddenly she didn't want to hear any more.

"Douglas, pass me that pot holder near you on the counter, will you?"

"Vanessa, I have purchased a ring for your approval."

Slowly she turned to look. In his left hand lay a

small black velvet box. From his right dangled the quilted pot holder. He stood and crossed the small kitchen, a look she had never seen in his eyes.

"Douglas, could we discuss this over dinner? I—I don't know what—"

"I'm burning with passion for you!" He threw his arms around Vanessa's waist.

"You are?" Her mouth was open in surprise.

"I'm mad about you. I can't stay away from you any longer! I can no longer hold myself back."

"You can't?" Her blue eyes opened wide.

"I can't live like this anymore. I can't stand it. I have to make you my wife."

"You do?" she asked, incredulous at his sudden transformation.

He fell on her in the narrow space in front of the stove. Vanessa tried to twist away from him as he grabbed for her. His elbow hit the handle of the saucepan filled with maple syrup, catapulting its sticky contents all over her slacks and down the front of his vest and trousers. They both jumped back, but too late.

"Oh, Douglas! Your suit is ruined!" She dabbed at the stains on his vest with a handy dish towel.

"No, not ruined. It's wash and wear. Everything will simply rinse out. The fabric dries in no time."

"Take off your clothes then and I'll rinse them out," she said, overjoyed at the unexpected diversion.

"But, Vanessa..." Douglas was actually blushing.

"I have a bathrobe you can wear. You jump in the shower and wash off the syrup. I'll rinse out your pants. Then I'll clean up. The crepes will hold and by the time we finish eating, your pants will be dry. You

can't drive all the way back to New Jersey with maple
syrup all over your clothes.''

"I suppose you're right," he answered reluctantly.
"I hate to be sticky." Vanessa was not surprised.

She led the abashed Douglas to the bedroom and
gave him the white terry-cloth bathrobe from the Hotel Georges V.

She returned to the kitchen and rinsed out his pants
in the sink. As she worked she thought of what she
would say to him. There really was no way to tell
someone nicely that you didn't care to marry him. To
tell Douglas the truth—that he was dull to the point of
giving her sleeping sickness—was out of the question.
She had to smile in disbelief when she thought of his
unanticipated change from Mr. Bloodless to Mr.
Hyde—she would never have thought he had any passion in him at all! Imagine, he had created an entire
scenario of which she had been blithely unaware, only
turning on the physical when he thought he had her
close to the altar. She wondered what Douglas would
say if he knew how she had spent Christmas, lying in
Jacques's muscular arms, transported on wings of ecstasy by his gentle hands. On a voyage of search for
hidden treasure. The prize had been the discovery of
parts of her body that had been so long hidden even
she had not known they existed until his probing
tongue had found them. An unexpected tear rolled
down her cheek. She brushed it away with the back of
her hand.

"The shower is free, Vanessa." Douglas stood at he
doorway of the kitchen in the fluffy white robe, a
patch of skin on each thin leg visible between black

socks and maroon garters. She realized she had been staring at the garters.

"I'll be right out. Make yourself a drink."

Jacques was stopped by the doorman, who made him wait while he went into a cubby off the lobby and rang Apartment 10D. Apparently Vanessa said she would see him because the doorman admitted him without another word. He rested the large pale blue box he carried on the floor of the elevator and loosened the lumberman's jacket he wore. Too hot in the building. He was used to the cool of the loft. He hoped she would like his gift. He *knew* she would. He had thought of her immediately when Chang had told him the neighbors in Weston had a large litter of cats they wanted to get rid of. Cats and zucchini—you couldn't give them away in the country.

He still distrusted her, he knew. But she mesmerized him. The way she smelled, like early spring flowers. Those penetrating ice-blue eyes. She was such a delightful combination of sophistication and innocence. He would never have suspected she had been married if she had not told him so herself. It was as if he himself had initiated her into the mysteries of making love. He hadn't met a woman like that in a long time....

When Bauman had called on Christmas night, confirming what he had already begun to suspect—that her visit was "strictly business" even though it had led to the bedroom—he had been so angry he'd wanted to kill her. Lucky for her she had already left for town. The anger had lasted—he was still angry—but some-

thing else had been working on him. He had come to
realize that despite the motivations that apparently
had brought her to him, he no longer cared. He wanted
her now. Something special and living existed between
them. He recognized it. He wanted it to grow.

No woman who had responded to him the way she
had that fantastic afternoon could be getting what she
needed from Murdoch. Mental stimulation, maybe.
Social niceties, perhaps. The right invitations to the
right parties. He himself didn't care about parties, but
if that's what she wanted, Jacques could do all that for
her. And then he could do more, so much more. She
had seen that clearly. That's why she had continued to
call and leave messages, even after he had deliberately
ignored her attempts to get in touch with him. Oh,
he'd been angry. But now he was willing—no, now he
was eager—to start again with her. He had been actually afraid she wouldn't see him and so he hadn't
called before coming over. He realized how tense he
felt as he walked down the hall to her apartment.

He rang the bell to 10D. He heard her footsteps in
the entrance foyer. A unfamiliar ball of apprehension
clutched his stomach. He smiled at his teen-age
nerves.

"Can I help you?" asked a bespectacled man in a
white bathrobe. Jacques looked dumbly from his in-
quiring face to the number on the apartment door.

"Is—is this Mrs. VanderPoel's apartment?" he
asked at last.

"Yes, she's in the shower. Is this package for her?"
He reached an arm out for the pale turquoise box.
"I'll take it."

"I...uh..."

"Hold on just a minute." The man took the box from Jacques's arm and carried it back into the apartment, out of his sight. Jacques saw he wore maroon garters. He returned a moment later holding his wallet. He handed Jacques a dollar bill.

"Who's it from?"

"Huh?" Jacques staring down at the dollar lying in his hand.

"I said, who's the package from?"

"I...uh..."

"Oh, all right," groaned the man in the bathrobe, his voice heavy with disgust. He pulled another bill from the wallet and thrust it into Jacques's hand. "You people really are robbers."

"I don't know, mister. I just deliver 'em. The card's probably inside. Hey, thanks for the tip." Jacques turned on his heel and walked quickly down the hall. "So long, bathrobe man," he called, but the door to 10D had already slammed shut.

Three elderly ladies entered the descending elevator on the seventh floor. His red hair towered over them. One with thick glasses and lavender hair looked up and down at his lumberjacket and paint-smeared blue jeans.

"Delivery people are requested to ride the service elevator, young man," she sniffed.

"I'll know better next time, ma'am." He smiled politely and moved to the back of the car. He felt like putting a fist through the wall, but there was no reason to take out his bad humor on the three frail birds who stood there. From his height he could look down into the neat parts that divided three shiny pink scalps.

"Did you see the ring, Crystal?"

"I saw it. Lovely. Mavis told me it's one and a half carats. She's a lucky girl."

"It's not so big," whined the next. "But he's a nice boy, steady. Good job. She's a lucky girl."

"*He's* the lucky one. She'll make him a nice wife," said the third. "If that's what she wants," she added doubtfully.

"You don't sound so enthusiastic, Lena."

"Oh, I'm happy, I suppose. She *should* be married again. Twenty-nine is too young to be a widow, but—"

Jacques's ears perked up.

"But what?" asked the one in thick glasses.

"He's not enough man for Vanessa," she said decisively.

"A girl needs security," began the first. The woman tottered out when the doors slid open at the lobby. The rest of her reply was lost to Jacques. He stood stunned in the elevator. Three pairs of matchstick legs crossed the marble floor and took seats on the long couch that faced the entrance door, settling in to watch the evening show of people crossing the lobby.

Vanessa showered and changed into the paisley caftan. How could she get Douglas to go home without giving him dinner? Headache? Arranged phone call from Maynard? She eyed the telephone thoughtfully. No, she'd have to bite the bullet. She'd have to feed him, flatter him, and tell him that she could not marry him. She'd rather have no one if she couldn't have Jacques. Did women still enter the convent? Could she tell Douglas she was going to join a cloistered order of nuns and pray for the sins of the world? She smiled in spite of herself. Douglas was so serious he would probably believe her.

When she went out into the living room, her eye spotted the new box immediately. The pale blue color, the ruby-red ribbon, were unmistakably from Tiffany's. This was going to be more awkward than she had anticipated; it simply was not in her character to accept an expensive gift from a man she was about to ease out of her apartment and her life.

"This box was just delivered," said Douglas.

"I don't think I should take any presents from you now, Douglas," she began.

"It's not from me. A delivery boy just dropped it off. I had to give him two dollars," he added plaintively.

Vanessa crossed the room and picked up the box, shaking it gently. "I'll pay you back," she said. Her fingers tore at the red ribbon. She removed the top and a single piece of tissue paper. At the bottom of the deep box, tucked into a corner, a tiny white kitten slept curled up in a ball no bigger than a large apple.

"Ye gods," she gasped. "It's a cat!" She reached a long-fingered hand into the box and extracted the furry ball. The kitten opened one pale eye and looked at her without curiosity. It twitched its pink nose and went back to sleep in her hand.

"That animal is only a few weeks old," said Douglas. "Who would have sent it? What an impractical gift."

His remark dispelled any lingering notion that the kitten might have been from him. That left only one possible person.

"Maynard would have," she said. "Only Maynard would send something like that in a big box from Tiffany's. He knows I'm mad at him and that's exactly how he'd try to make peace. I love the little thing." She stroked its angora neck gently. "But I'm still angry."

"That fop! I don't know what you see in him. He makes my skin crawl."

"Douglas, Maynard's my best friend. I'll have to ask you never to talk like that about him again."

"Well, after you and I are married, I'll have to ask *you* not to see him again. It just isn't done."

"*What* isn't done?" So Douglas Finer was not so nice after all. And wasn't he getting feisty all of a sudden, assuming all sorts of rights over her, and she hadn't even responded to his extremely lukewarm proposal. Quick anger began to simmer in the pit of her stomach. Perhaps extricating herself was not going to be as difficult as she had imagined earlier.

"You know, hanging around with someone like him. It isn't natural, Vanessa." He lowered his voice to a whisper as if to tell her some shocking truth that she was still too young to know. "He's not a real man."

"Oh, Maynard's not a real man, is that what you think? To me he's as much a man as you are and perhaps a great deal more so! Maynard is a true gentleman and what's more, *he* knows how to live and let live. He doesn't go around criticizing *your* life-style. I can't believe you, who's been around, who travels all over the world, could have such an attitude about him. How could I *not* see him? My God, Douglas, I work with him every day of my life!''

"You'll quit your job."

"What?" She heard her voice go up half an octave.

"Of course. I can't imagine you'd commute. I thought you could get a little part-time job in New Jersey."

"At your aunt's frame-it-yourself shop in Summit, no doubt," she said acidly.

"Well, yes. That *is* the art business, after all. She could use someone with your experience," he went on benignly, blissfully unaware of Vanessa's rising temper.

"Douglas, the *art* business, what a put-down! This is going to come as a big surprise to you, but I'm not interested in your idea of a suitable 'little' job for me. I'm not interested in living in New Jersey. *And* I don't plan to marry you!'' She grabbed the drip-dry gray pants from where they hung over a radiator and threw them at him. They fell in a damp heap at his feet. "Put these on and start commuting back to New Jersey—one way!"

"They're still wet," he whined.

"They'll suit you perfectly."

He picked up the fallen trousers and scuttled into the bedroom. Vanessa stormed into the kitchen and threw all the crepes into the trash. She spied Douglas's gray jacket still hanging on the back of the dining-room chair. She put the ring box in one pocket without opening it.

On Thursday her father and his bride arrived in New York. Vanessa was unable to meet them at the airport, but they had called from Miami and made arrangements to come to her apartment for cocktails before going out to dinner at a restaurant she was to choose.

When the bell rang, she was putting the finishing touches on her makeup, surprised at how nervous she was. She wondered if her father would like the apartment: He hadn't been to New York since she had redecorated and she tried to see the rooms' severe lines with his eyes. Would they tell too much about her? Would the somber tones make him worry? In the past he had always stayed with her and Andrew, but this visit he was stopping at the Plaza with Marie, his new wife. At first Vanessa had been surprised at the arrangements, but she told herself that they were on their honeymoon, after all.

They stood on the doorstep expectantly. Marie was a surprise to Vanessa, not at all what she had pictured. Her plump face and arms were tanned golden from the Caribbean sun. Around her eyes white lines were etched into the skin—lines from laughter, not concern. She looked as if she baked her own bread.

Her father, as thin as Marie was plump, seemed rested and content. His nut-brown skin was the picture of health. Right away she noticed that they touched each other a lot, little pats on the arm or on the back of the hand. Her heart ached to see her father so happy. He had been alone for nearly twenty years.

They brought in a gigantic black box from an elegant shop on Bonaire whose name she readily recognized.

After she had prepared cocktails for the three of them, they sat in the living room and admired her collection of lithographs in their antique frames. Vanessa gave them the cut-glass fruit bowl she had picked out the previous Monday. Marie offered her the shiny black box from Bonaire. She opened it and found four hand-appliqued pillows that depicted natives at work on the islands. Their brilliant colors contrasted strongly with the muted gray tones of the living room. She propped them up against the leather couch behind where Marie and her father sat close together. She had no choice; she wanted to show her appreciation of the gift. But the pillows were so riotous, so gay and naive, they looked strange in the clean, modern lines of the room.

She basked in the glow of her father's presence after such a long time without seeing him. She listened attentively as he and Marie told her of mutual acquaintances in Cleveland, but all the while she searched vainly for an opportunity to insert Jacques's name into the conversation. She wished he were there with the three of them. Jacques would like Marie; she was the warm and loving mother he had never had. Her father would like Jacques, she had no doubt whatsoever. And Jacques would find her father knowledgeable and interested in his work, as his own father had never been.

Always with her was the longing that he would show one small sign that he cared for her. She watched the newlyweds exchange eloquent, silent glances of affection. When her father stood and held Marie's coat, she saw the quick squeeze he gave her shoulders. She wanted to go to her bedroom, close the door behind her, and cry.

Instead she put on her coat and they went to dinner at the Oak Room of the Plaza Hotel. She chose the restaurant because it was convenient for Marie and her father and because she remembered that fresh oysters and clams were always on the menu there, delicacies that one could seldom order in Cleveland.

After dessert she and Marie went to the ladies' room. Marie appeared to have something on her mind. Her usually placid face stared at Vanessa in the mirror.

"How do you feel about your father and me? About our remarriage?" she asked at last.

Vanessa was surprised. "Nothing but happy for you both. Do you mean, am I jealous that you might want to replace my mother? Not at all! Marie, I barely remember my mother now. I was only ten when she died, you know. My father has been alone all these years. I want him to have a wife. I want him to find happiness with someone and you obviously love him as much as he loves you, Marie. I'm pleased you are married, really pleased."

"And why aren't you remarried, Vanessa? As I understand it, you've been alone for more than three years now. Isn't that right? Don't make the same mistake I did. I waited much too long. It's not natural for a woman to live alone."

"I—I haven't found the right man," she said, embarrassed at the dearth of creativity that impelled her to respond with such a trite phrase. *I've found the right man* she wanted to say, *but he hasn't found me and it looks like he never will.*

"Don't wait for one to fall in your lap. Go after what you want!" Marie smiled enigmatically and her eyes sparkled with an almost fanatical resolve. She was obviously a take-charge person.

Vanessa combed her hair and thought about what Marie had just said. Lena had given her the same message in different words not too long ago.

"How long were you widowed, Marie?"

"Too long. My children were young. I was busy with their needs, with making ends meet. I was so busy I didn't have time for myself." She applied her lipstick as she talked, making a grimace and pressing her lips together firmly. "Finally I got smart and decided to be in charge of my own destiny. Good men don't just pop out of the woodwork, you know. A woman has to work at finding one. If that's what she wants," she added, looking pointedly at Vanessa in the mirror.

"Is that what you did?"

"You bet! The first time I saw your father I went right up to him at the summer theater during intermission and I said, 'I'd like to get to know you.'"

Vanessa stared at Marie's reflection in the mirror, her blue eyes wide with wonder.

"You're kidding! What did he say?"

"I think he answered, 'That sounds like a good idea to me,' or some such words. The rest, as they say, is history."

"Marie! That's beautiful."

"So don't let the grass grow under your feet, girl. There's too much of your life left to live. Quality of life, that's what we all want. Forget the rest, throw caution to the winds and grab what you want."

"I'll remember what you said, Marie," Vanessa answered. A new gleam of determination shone in her blue eyes. They returned to the table in the Oak Room where Vanessa's father awaited them. Vanessa's cheeks were flushed.

As soon as she unlocked the door to her apartment Vanessa rushed to the answering machine. No one had called, not even Maynard, despite the gift of the kitten, who was presently locked in the bathroom. She dialed Jacques's answering service first. The same bored voice told her in nearly unintelligible Brooklynese that Mr. Power was out of town. She punched out the numbers for the house in Connecticut.

"Yes, I told him your message, missy. Long time ago."

"Thank you, Mrs. Chang."

No matter that he was avoiding her. No matter that he hadn't called or returned her calls to him. There was always the gallery opening the next night. She had no intention of making the same mistakes Lena and Marie had made. She loved Jacques, even if he had abused her affection, made her sick with worry and despair. No matter how his not calling after Christmas had hurt her. She didn't care. Nothing changed her love for him. If Jacques refused to see her ever again— well, she would deal with that rejection when it happened. *If* it happened. And if he rejected her, she'd still love him, she knew. As Lena still loved her dead long-ago lover. Vanessa had read the faithful love that continued to burn in Lena's pale eyes when she spoke of him.

Chapter Nine

Vanessa stood outside the SoHo gallery. She had paid the driver and the taxi was gone. Couples went in the blank, brick facade, pair after pair of glittering couples, anxious to be seen at a major opening, anxious to drop their money or at least the names of their famous acquaintances. Each time the door of the gallery opened she heard the buzz of voices waft out into the crisp winter air. She needed one more minute to compose herself. No doubt Jacques was already inside. She had purposely arrived late and the scheduled cocktail party would be two thirds over by the time she steeled her nerves enough to walk through the door, hand written invitation in clammy hand.

She tried out what she would say to him, the right approach. She wanted to be nice, but she was angry. She wished him to know she was angry, but she didn't want to be hostile. She told herself she deserved an explanation for his behavior, but she knew in her heart that she was poised to believe almost anything he might say. In truth, she did not know how to handle their meeting and she was afraid. She pressed her lips together and a worried frown creased her high forehead.

At last she knew she had to go into the gallery and get it over with. She arranged the collar of the soft silk blouse one last time. She patted her frosted hair. She took a deep breath and entered the plate-glass door.

Perhaps seventy-five people wrapped in fur and gold filled the humming room. Perhaps two hundred. She never knew. She saw only one. His red hair jumped out at her across the sleek coiffures of the idle rich who had come down to be part of the trendy SoHo scene. A hand took her coat. Another hand shoved a plastic glass of white wine in her empty one. She sipped automatically and discarded the glass when she discovered its contents tasted of ashes on her tongue. She made her way slowly through the crowd, oblivious of the oil paintings brightly lit on all four walls, oblivious of the short young man in gray flannel who attempted to start a conversation with her.

At last she was twenty feet from him. His back was to her, his head inclined in conversation with a dark woman with enormous black eyes and a hard, thin mouth. She knew this had to be the Middle Eastern dealer Antonio had told her of, the owner of the gallery.

A stunning blonde whose face was vaguely familiar to Vanessa approached Jacques from his left and spoke to him, laying a perfectly manicured long fingernail on his wool sleeve as she did so. Vanessa watched the wiry curls at the back of his neck as he turned in response to the blonde's question. She recognized the mask of irritation that lowered over his craggy face. The blonde persisted and he turned his head further to her to answer. Vanessa met his eyes across the space that separated them. Her heart stopped. For a long moment their eyes locked in silent appraisal. *I love you, I love you, I love you,* she repeated mutely like a mantra, certain his soul heard the words hers whispered across the cosmos.

He placed his arm around the blonde's bare shoulder, leaned down to whisper in her perfectly shaped ear, and smiling, he turned his back.

A sharp pain went through Vanessa. She stared at the back of Jacques's red head and watched him as he inclined intimately toward the blonde. His large hand lightly caressed the tanned skin of the woman's bare arm. Vanessa felt her high cheekbones begin to burn and she was certain that her face was crimson from the public snub she had just received. How dare he! She hadn't come this far just to have Jacques Power turn his back on her.

Feeling so enraged that the festive gallery blurred before her blue eyes, Vanessa crossed the few feet which still separated her from Jacques and plucked at his sleeve, no longer interested in caution.

"I want to talk to you," she stated boldly, interrupting the blonde in midsentence.

"So talk." His green eyes appraised her coolly.

"Not here. Privately."

"You can talk here. What's-her-name here won't pay attention. She only listens to herself anyway."

The blonde pouted and opened her mouth to object.

"Run along and get yourself a drink," he ordered. She obeyed without another word.

"Not here."

"Come into the office, then. The owner won't mind."

She followed his broad back through the crowd. He led her to a disorderly room, then stepped aside, indicating that she should enter first. He closed the door behind himself and leaned his lanky frame against it. To keep others out or her in? Suddenly, she had no idea what to say. She didn't have to worry. He spoke first.

"You look very beautiful. I—I like your blouse. It suits your coloring." He sounded nervous, unlike his usual confident self.

"Thank you." The unexpected compliment put her off guard and in a word defused much of her anger. How mercurial he was! One minute turning his back on her most hurtfully, the next flattering her and devouring her with those hungry green eyes.

"Come here. There's something wrong with one of the buttons," he said softly.

She looked down at the front of the blouse.

"I don't see anything wrong," she said, bewildered.

"You wouldn't be able to see it. Come here, I'll fix it."

She crossed the small room in two steps. His hands touched the thin silk of the blouse. She looked down at his wrists while he did something with the offending button. Red hairs grew from the skin. She longed to kiss the bone just showing beneath the cuff of his shirt. Memories of those strong hands on her body haunted her.

Slowly she inhaled his distinctive scent, tilting her head imperceptibly closer to his red hair to more fully enjoy his fragrance. She couldn't get enough of him in her nostrils. The air in the small room was warm. Jacques's breath lulled and warmed her like the caress of tepid water. He lifted his eyes and she felt them on her, but she could not look at him as he looked at her. Her vision was blurred by the intensity of her feelings. She was magnetically drawn to touch his flesh with her hands or her mouth or with her whole body. Her senses were drugged. When she raised an arm to gently brush the bone of his wrist, her hand was heavy. At the feel of his skin on her hand, her knees went weak. It was she who moved toward him and offered him her mouth.

He kissed her and he parted the rustling fabric and inserted his large hands inside the blouse to cover the silky skin of her breasts beneath the tiny intricate pleats. He had undone four of the buttons under the guise of adjusting just one. He kissed her neck where the blue veins were palpitating and he kissed the hollow of her throat. She wrapped her hands around his neck and pressed her breasts into the warmth of his palms. She pulled his avid mouth to hers, swaying with a desire to be taken wholly. While they kissed he slowly opened the blouse fully and slipped his arms around her waist, spreading his long fingers on the smooth skin of her back. He followed the lines of her back lovingly, seeking to take possession of her with his hands. He stepped slightly away and her breasts were freed to his gaze. For a long moment his eyes rested on their fullness. He returned his lips to the hollow of her throat where the skin was softest and most tender and where she knew her heartbeat echoed.

She let his mouth and hands glide over her skin, resting here, lingering there, bowing her head over his red hair when he placed his mouth on her throat, which held the words she had sought him out to tell him, twisting her fingers in the wiry red hair when he lowered his lips to her breasts. She moaned. The noise startled her in the quiet room. Behind the thin door to the office, inches away, the party continued. She was oblivious. She heard his breath come more heavily as his blood grew richer.

"Oh, God," he groaned in a tortured whisper, turning his head slightly to rest his cheek in the hollow between her breasts and speaking into the flesh.

She felt the words as well as heard them, his breath warm and moist on her skin, caressing the space between her breasts as would a salty, damp breeze from the summer sea.

"Oh, God, I've never wanted anyone so much." She shivered where the dewy exhalation from his lips brushed her skin. She was unable to answer. She pushed her fingers through his hair, feeling its resilient texture on the tender inner skin along the knuckles, pushed them over and over, watching the glistening red strands flatten at her touch and spring back vibrantly after her trembling hand had passed.

His lips returned to one tight nipple and his tongue circled it slowly, teasing, drawing a fine line around it with the tip, as if the tongue were an extension of his artist's hand, a calligraphy brush painting on thin

Japanese rice paper, impelling the darkened skin to an impervious hardness.

She ached with desire for him, a welcome, growing pain that made her want to weep to expel the shaking fullness of her heart.

He slid one hand down her thigh and under the black skirt. The tissue of her stockings hissed as his fingers traveled up the gossamer nylon that clung to her limbs. She heard the fabric sing under his touch. He cupped his hand behind one hip and pushed her to his muscular legs so that their two bodies pressed firmly together from knee to lips and they held each other tightly in the still room.

He kissed one earlobe gently. "How did this happen?" he said in a low voice, talking more to himself than to her. "How did I ever allow this to happen?"

Suddenly he wrenched his arms away from her pliant body and placed his hands on her shoulders, holding her an arm's length away from him. His grip tightened painfully. His strong hands hurt the bones of her arms despite the protection of the shoulder pads of the wool jacket that now hung loosely open, as did the silk blouse. Her white breasts, freed from her clothes and from the warm touch of his hands, glowed pallidly in the harsh light of the office.

"You're cruel, you know," he said in a voice choked with raw need. "Why are you doing this now?"

" *You're* cruel," she answered. "Why did you stop?" Her voice was a hoarse whisper. A sudden chill filled her limbs and made her shiver. She covered her breasts with her hands, crossing her arms protectively in front of them. She felt the painful tension of unsatisfied want. Her nerves were unbearably keen and awake. Her blood was in turmoil. Her swollen lips were half-open with desire and the muscles of one thigh were in a fine tremor.

"I know what you're here for and I'm not playing anymore. I've had it with being used." There was no anger in his voice, just a note of painful resignation. A film of determination closed off his green eyes.

"What are you talking about? How am I using *you*?"

Jacques let out a short, mirthless laugh. "That's a good one, 'How do I use you, let me count the ways.' Let's see the new jewelry."

"What new jewelry? What do you mean?" A roar was growing in Vanessa's ears. Somewhere in the back of her mind a new understanding of the fine line between passion and pain, between consummate love and burning hate, began to dawn. He could manipulate her totally. Bring her to the point of making love with him *here*, two thin inches of plywood from a hundred strangers. Without heed for when or where, without thought for anything but the desire that lay between them like an unleashed tiger. Bring her to the edge of insanity and then drop a sheet of icy disdain between them as easily as other men inhaled or pushed their hair back from their brows or hailed a taxi. She felt totally naked and vulnerable before him. She *was* half naked. She looked down at her arms across her bare breasts in surprise, as if just awakening from a dream, a fantasy dream suddenly turning into a nightmare. She pulled the silk blouse closed to cover her pointed breasts and began to fumble with the buttons. Her fingers felt like rubber.

He began to speak. She didn't want to listen, but there was no way to escape the low, harsh words.

"I've known women like you before. Classy women, very respectable. Dames like Celia Bauman. A nice quiet husband who works himself into an early grave so she can have all the comforts she wants and meanwhile he never suspects she has a little something going on the side for excitement. What's more exciting than a bona fide, antisocial artist? Come to me when you want good sex and then go home to the suburbs to lead your real life. That ought to go over great at the Larchmont Women's Club. Think of the stories you'll be able to tell the girls over luncheon. Or did I pick the wrong town? Where's it going to be— Darien? Short Hills?" He listed the elegant suburbs of New York City.

He grabbed her roughly by the left hand and stared at her fingers. A look of surprise crossed his angry face.

"Where's the ring? The one-and-a-half carats?" he snapped with venom.

"*What* ring?" He wasn't, he couldn't be talking about Douglas! He didn't even know about Douglas.

"Don't play dumb; you know what ring! The one Mr. Bathrobe just gave you. Mr. Security. Mr. Respectability." His voice was low with controlled anger.

"How do you know about *him*?" she asked, genuinely perplexed. The roar in her ears grew, but not loud enough to drown out the contemptuous sting of his words.

"What difference does it make? You're welcome to all the men you want in your life, even if they don't have any blood in their veins. If that's what you're into, go ahead. Don't imagine that it matters to *me*. Just don't think you can add me to the list." He turned away from her.

"Hey, wait a minute!" She grabbed his upper arm and made him turn to look at her.

"I'm not going to take this from you!" she spat in a low voice, now acutely aware of the party going on a few feet away. "Did I ask *you* what that whore was doing in your studio? Did I ask *you* whose clothes you lent me on Christmas Day?" She stuffed her blouse into the waistband of her skirt. "What the hell makes you think you can push *me* around like this? After you went to bed with me you never bothered to call. You never tried to get in touch with me. You won't answer my phone calls. You act like I'm some kind of tramp that can be thrown out with the bilge water. Well, I've got news for you, Mr. Picasso, Mr. High and Mighty Big Shot Artist. I'm not a tramp! I am not a one-night-stand! Nobody walks out on me like that! I like myself too much to put up with your ego and your *sensitivity*. Go back to your groupies and your models-for-hire! That kind of woman is obviously the only kind you've ever dealt with. That's the only thing you can handle! You don't know a good thing when you see it. I feel sorry for you. You wouldn't know what to do with a woman who cares about you if she walked up and bit you on the rear. I never wanted anything from you, not what *you* seem to think I did anyway. And what I thought I wanted before I'm certainly not interested in now, believe me! There are much easier ways to get pleasure out of living than hitting my head against a brick wall, although I must admit I'm looking forward to how good it's going to feel when I stop. Get out of my way!''

She pushed him aside and stormed out the office door.

Vanessa toyed with the glass of white wine, which left wet rings on the table before her. Why was Maynard so late? She looked around the crowded and noisy dining room of The Brasserie. Perhaps it had not been a good idea to ask Maynard to meet her there; even at midnight so many people were lined up at the top of the stairs waiting to be seated that she felt painfully conspicuous sitting alone at the table with only a glass of cold white wine before her. She checked her wristwatch. If Maynard didn't arrive in five minutes, she decided that she would leave. She glanced up at the street entrance just in time to see him come through the revolving door and ease his way to the front of the disgruntled people milling there. His lean face glowed with the dark tan he had acquired skiing. Funny, she hadn't realized how handsome he still remained despite his age. No wonder so many women continued to pursue him avidly, only to be disappointed when he evinced no interest in their attentions. He had inadvertently broken more than one heart.

She waved and caught his eye. He made his way to the table against the wall where she sat and bent to kiss her cheek.

"Just a glass of wine," he told the waiter. "I've already eaten, my dear. I am sorry to be so tardy, but it was not easy getting away from the dinner party and since you told me to come alone, I had to see Antonio home. How can you eat so late in the evening? It gives me terrible heartburn. But, of course, I am a decade or so older than you."

"Or so. I'll have the mushroom and spinach salad and another glass of wine," she told the waiter.

"All right, I'll concede two decades older. Now, Vanessa, what are we doing here at midnight?"

"It's the only nice place I could think of that serves food at this hour, aside from the singles bars."

"I don't mean *where*. I mean *why*," he said irritably.

"Maynard, please don't be mean to me," she replied. Against her will she burst into tears. Maynard jumped up from his chair and sat down just as quickly. He reached across the table and patted her hand in staccato rhythm.

"Dear girl! What *is* the matter? Oh, don't cry. What *ever* is the matter? Are you sick? Is your father all right? Please don't cry, you'll muss your mascara. People will wonder what's wrong. Oh, dear girl, please stop and tell me what the problem is." He pulled a spotless silk handkerchief from his breast pocket and passed it across the table to her.

"Maynard, I swore I wouldn't cry. I'm so sorry." Vanessa made an enormous effort to get herself under control. "You know I don't wear mascara."

"Don't keep me in suspense, then. Get to it. You didn't drag me to this prom-night eatery just to talk about cosmetics, did you?" Although the words were gruff, his voice had turned gentle. He waited patiently for her to stop crying long enough to explain.

"It's... it's..." Her eyes filled with tears again.

"It's Jacques Power, *n'est ce pas*?" he finished the sentence for her.

"Yes," she said in a small voice. "How do you know?"

"You think I grew to be this old without learning something about people? I saw there was something between you. Anyone could see it."

"I spent Christmas with him at his place in the country. It was wonderful. He was wonderful. The whole time was the most magnificent experience I've ever had in my life."

"It was so wonderful that, in fact, you're crying your eyes out. Oh, spare me such ecstasy, dear Lord. 'Love's a disease—'"

"Yes, I know, 'but curable,'" she interrupted.

"I'm getting to be a boring old man. Do me a favor: Have me put out on an ice floe. If your little tryst was so wonderful, then what is the problem?"

"Well, after Christmas, I never heard from him. He didn't call, he didn't come to the atelier, he wouldn't return *my* calls. When I couldn't stand it anymore, I went to see him and he was unbearably cruel. I can't even talk about what happened. I just can't understand it. What went wrong? What have I done wrong?"

"Why do you think *you* did something wrong? Perhaps the fault lies with Power."

"I can't eat, I can't sleep. I cry all the time. I thought Jacques and I had something really, really special. Maynard, help me, what can I do?"

"Vanessa, you're no longer a child and you already know the answer to that question. You just need to hear old Maynard say it for you, isn't that right?"

"You mean I should forget him, don't you? Oh, Maynard, how can I forget him? I've never met a man like Jacques before. Do you think there's another woman involved? You told me he had a reputation—"

"And you didn't believe old Maynard. I must be losing my touch with you." He sighed and daintily wiped his lips with his napkin. "Eat your salad, you're looking quite gaunt, you know."

"I'm not hungry." She put down her fork. She had pushed the mushrooms to one side of the bowl and was now methodically piling them on the other side. "Yes, I believed you when you told me. But when I was with him, I thought it would be different; I thought I was someone special to him. Oh, I can't explain—you know what I'm talking about, don't you?"

"Certainly I do. I think he's a man in love."

"In love? With me?" she asked with a new and sudden note of hope in her voice.

"No, not with you, with himself. 'He fell in love at first sight and it's a passion to which he has always remained faithful.'"

"Who said that?"

"What does it matter? I have a million of them: 'The man who loves himself cannot be accused of promiscuity in his affections, but he is bound—'"

"Enough, Maynard. What about me? What shall I do?"

"Forget Power and your 'magnificent experience.'

Do something nice for Vanessa. You must take care of yourself first. If Jacques Power wants to let a woman like you slip through his fingers, that's his problem. But you be healthy—don't waste your time pining away for a cretin like him. *Imbécil*! *Tonto*!''

"Tonto? As in Heigh-ho-Silver?"

"*Tonto* is perfectly proper Spanish for 'fool.' I am studying Spanish, my dear. I have a little cassette I play each night as I cook dinner."

"Ah, yes, Antonio's influence. I'm happy for you, Maynard." It was her turn to pat his long hand.

"I know you are, Vanessa. You are a kind and thoughtful woman. Jacques Power hardly deserves the emotional energy you're expending on him, believe me."

"Thank you for the compliment, Maynard. You've always been my best fan," she told him with a soft smile.

"But *you* should be your best fan, Vanessa. You have to start indulging yourself. Take off that hair shirt you've been wearing ever since your husband died. *You* didn't kill him. You did everything anyone was able to do and you don't have any responsibility for what happened, you know that, don't you?"

"Yes, I know." She reluctantly agreed because she knew Maynard wanted her to believe what he said. As always, in her heart she felt she might have done more for Andrew. But she did not know what more she could have done. "Maynard, you don't seriously believe I go around punishing myself, wearing a hair shirt—isn't that what you said?"

"In effect, you do. You've closed yourself off from

other men to protect yourself from being hurt. Isn't depriving yourself of a man's love punishment? What do you want to do, build a funeral pyre for Andrew and throw yourself upon it? Because that's exactly how you are leading your life."

"No, no! You're wrong," she said quickly, shocked at his analysis of her. "What about Jacques? I let *him* get to me. I opened myself up completely to him and look what he did to me! That disproves your theory completely."

"*Au contraire*, my little one. I think it proves my theory admirably. You chose a totally unsuitable man upon whom to bestow your attentions, knowing full well the likelihood of heartbreak, so that afterward you'd be able to say, 'You see? He hurt me. It's better not to get involved.' Well?" He sat back and crossed his arms over his chest, a look of triumph on his angular features.

"Do you really think so?" Vanessa twirled the stem of the wineglass between her fingers. Maynard might be right. His theory appeared plausible. She had been warned about Jacques, there was no denying the fact, but she had been irresistibly drawn to him like a moth to its certain destruction in flame. She realized she'd hoped she'd be the one woman who could change Jacques's ways. Just as she'd hoped her cheerful nature would jolly Andrew out of his moodiness and his depressions. Chronic depression, she amended. Chronic depression—*not* vague and transitory depressions. Chronic even before Vanessa had met and dated and later married Andrew. In a flash of understanding, she saw herself as Maynard must have. "Oh, Lord, I believe you're right. Oh, Maynard." She looked down at the table dejectedly, unable to meet his eyes. "Maynard, I don't want to be like that. What can I do?"

"I have a plan. Promise me you'll do exactly as I tell you. No objections tolerated. Do you promise?"

"I have to hear your plan first," she hedged. Maynard's wild imagination was legendary. When she became aware of the sullen pout on his lips, she said, "Well, *if* it's not *too* crazy I'll go along."

"Wholehearted or not at all!" He leaned forward and whispered to her in a conspiratorial manner. "Have I ever, in all the years we've known each other, ever led you astray?"

"No, never," she admitted. "All right, what's the plan?" She exhaled a sigh of resignation, knowing she was about to fall down Alice's tunnel to Wonderland.

"You shall go away for a week or ten days. Go and relax, get a suntan, read some highly frivolous books, and generally recharge your batteries. While you're gone you'll forget that blankety-blank artist and maybe even meet the man of your dreams."

"Forget it, I can't afford it," she interjected.

"How do you know? Bauman's got his prints in house on time, thanks to you, and you're going to receive a big bonus plus a week off with pay for the extraordinary effort you made to keep Jacques Power happy."

If only you knew what an effort, she thought to herself. But all she said was "What makes you think Bauman will do all that for me?"

"He will. I'll see that he does. He'll do it. You know

as well as I that you've pulled Columbia out of the soup." Everything Maynard said was true and Vanessa was quite aware of it.

"Where could I go?" she objected. "It's the height of the season. I'd never get a hotel room anywhere I'd want to go. Besides, Maynard, even a nice bonus won't cover the expense of going someplace hot in the winter, you know that."

"Let *me* worry about that," said Maynard, his eyes twinkling mysteriously. "It won't cost you a cent."

"I couldn't take money from you, Maynard. What are you talking about?" she said quickly.

"It won't cost *me* a cent either. So it's final? You'll do it? You're making the right decision, dear. This is the first step in indulging yourself. Just the beginning of a wonderful life for you."

"You hedonist! But I can't go. I just remembered, what about my cat?"

"You don't have a cat! Stop looking for outs. You promised, you know."

"Yes, I do, a kitten. She came by messenger to my apartment the other day. Stop kidding me, Maynard. You left her there, didn't you?"

"Of course not, I hate cats. Besides, I'd never give an anonymous gift; it's not my nature."

"She was in a big blue Tiffany box, tied up in red satin ribbon. Maynard, she wasn't from you? Really?"

"I swear it. Ugh! And of course, you named the creature Tiffany."

"Of course. Anyway, you see I can't go. There's no one to take care of her," she said with finality.

"*I* will care for your animal. But I will not call her Tiffany and that is final."

As Maynard had promised, Bauman gave Vanessa a week off with pay and a generous bonus. Within the envelope he left on her desk she found a handwritten note. "You saved the company and my marriage. Thank you, Richard." Tears came to her eyes for him. She was pleased his financial problems were solved for the time being, but she doubted that she—or anyone—would salvage his marriage to the voracious Celia. Richard's wife would continue to spend and spend, bringing on the same crisis time after time until Bauman awoke to what was going on or Celia found a richer daddy to indulge her caviar tastes.

On a late January Saturday morning she found herself sitting between Maynard and Antonio da Silva in the back seat of a chauffer-driven navy-blue limousine on the expressway to Kennedy International Airport. In the trunk lay Vanessa's suitcase packed with clothes for the tropics. At her feet sat the blue box from Tiffany's, but the sonamed cat rested in Maynard's lap, softly purring as he scratched the white fur behind her pink ears.

"She's not so bad, I admit. She seems to like me a bit, don't you, sweet little thing?" asked Maynard.

"Some cat-hater *you* are, Maynard," said Vanessa. "Are you certain you want to bring her all the way out to Long Island for the weekend?"

"Everyone will love her, won't they, Antonio?"

Antonio nodded his agreement. "Here are the keys to the condominium in Manzanillo. When you arrive at Las Hadas, go directly to the office—not to the hotel desk, but the condominium office. Give them this letter and they will take care of you. There's a kitchen in the apartment and groceries are available in the village, but of course you may take all your meals in the hotel if you care to. There's a lovely open-air restaurant overlooking the swimming pools where you will see magnificent native parrots and flowers such as your eyes have never beheld."

"I can't believe what's happening!" exclaimed Vanessa. "How could you arrange to borrow the apartment on such short notice?"

"Don't you know," asked Antonio, "that women will do almost anything for their decorators? Anyway, the owners of the apartment have gone to Buenos Aires for an extended visit to one of their married children. The place was vacant and it was simplicity itself to make the arrangements. You are not to worry—it will be as if you are in your own home. You understand, this is only a weekend place, rather crude. There will be no servants."

"I think I will manage, Antonio." Vanessa giggled.

"It's good to hear you laugh, my dear," said Maynard, looking out the window at the slush-filled Van Wyck Expressway. "And it's about time."

Vanessa bade the men good-bye and boarded the plane, seeking her seat in the economy section, only to be told that she was to be a first-class passenger. Maynard had checked her in at the ticket counter while she waited at another desk for her Mexican tourist card. It was just like Maynard to surprise her by

218   *Canvas of Passion*

paying the difference in fare so that she would ride in first class. She accepted a glass of champagne before lunch and wrote him a letter of thanks on the stationery the flight attendant provided at her request. The airplane followed the sun to Guadalajara where she passed through customs and then changed to a smaller jet for the twenty-five-minute flight bound for the town of Manzanillo on the tropical Pacific Coast of Mexico. She watched out the window of the jet in disbelief when the aircraft drifted low over the pounding surf to make a perfect landing on the oceanside runway. The sun was just dropping into the Pacific with a dazzling display of fireworks. Darkness fell on the narrow highway lined with coconut palms as an apparently springless taxi raced her south toward the resort complex of Las Hadas. When the driver turned off the road and began a nerveracking ascent up a twisting cobblestone road in the inky tropical blackness, she held on to the seat to keep herself upright and concentrated on the few vine-covered houses illuminated by the headlights of the old car as it climbed. Thus she was totally unprepared when a final twist in the road revealed a vision of turreted white splendor seemingly torn from the pages of *The Arabian Nights*. Vanessa gasped in surprise.

"Las Hadas, senorita. The most splendid resort in all of Mexico," the driver bragged.

"I believe you!" she answered.

Subtly hidden spotlights in the lush jungle growth cleverly illuminated a complex of white arabic buildings fashioned to recreate a dense hillside village. Snowy clusters of balconies and turrets climbed the rugged cliffs and hugged steep rocks overlooking a serene cove. On the distant opposite shore of a wide bay, the white lights of the port of Manzanillo sparkled in the balmy night air, heavy with the sweet redolence of tropical blossoms. She smiled inwardly at the paradox of life: Only a month before she had never even heard of Manzanillo and here it lay before her—a fantasy paradise spread richly at her feet, free for the taking for the next nine days. Las Hadas shimmered before her, a dreamlike mixture of architectural and natural splendors. She wished for only one more ingredient to fulfill the perfection of Las Hadas—someone with whom to share its stunning beauty.

Jacques Power liked women. He also liked pristine new tubes of paint and spicy Chinese food. He consumed all three with equal if fleeting passion. When he wanted any of them, he rang up the appropriate number and a knock at his door would fulfill his whims with alacrity. Like all rich or famous men, he had discovered long ago that somewhere someone existed to supply any demand.

But lately he'd tired of the game. He hadn't spoken to another woman since the blond starlet his agent had arranged for him to escort to the opening of his new show, the girl with the vacant eyes, which adequately reflected the cotton wool between her ears where her brains should have been. He hadn't painted anything new since his father's chaotic pre-Christmas visit and his fingers itched to return to the half-finished canvas on the wooden easel across the room. Yet everytime he picked up a sable brush he thought of twenty insignificant errands to run and he laid his paints aside once more. And he'd lost his taste for Chinese food, even Mrs. Chang's fiery Hunan specialties.

He sat at one end of a trestle table in the SoHo loft, white containers of Chinese takeout spread in a half circle before him. He picked disinterestedly. Outside a heavy snow was falling and he wondered if he should bother with the drive to Connecticut the next day. At his side was the latest copy of an architectural magazine, which he glanced at between bites of food. He relished the silence of the studio after his father's tumultuous visit.

With a twinge he thought again that he hadn't painted anything worthwhile since before Christmas, since he'd begun to print those damn lithographs at Columbia Atelier. The whole job had taken much longer than he'd anticipated when he signed the contract with Bauman. Perhaps he should have taken Bauman's suggestion and allowed Vanessa to do all the technical work for him. Her work really was excellent, he admitted to himself. She would have done a magnificent job on his prints, and in a fraction of the time it had taken Jacques. But, no, he still preferred to operate his own way. He didn't need her help. She'd turned out just like all the others—she too had wanted something from him. He had hoped, had thought, had been certain, she was different for a while. She had fooled him. Not any longer, though. Why had she been so interested in the outcome of the prints? Was she a part owner of the atelier? What was in it for her? Idly he wondered what the story was between her and

Richard Bauman. She'd certainly done her best to save the contract for Bauman. Above and beyond the call of duty, he'd say. She didn't seem the type to be involved with a married man, but then who could tell these days? Jacques knew more than one married woman who had made her availability palpably clear to him. But Bauman, that simpering idiot! How could she? No way could he picture them together. But he knew one thing: She'd go to bed with a client to save the account!

Jacques swore under his breath and slammed a fist on the bare table. The paper containers jumped. She had seemed so sincere! He'd never had an experience like Christmas Day with any woman in his forty years. When they made love that long Christmas afternoon he'd really thought he'd found the right woman at last. But when she'd mentioned the prints, when Bauman had called later, so nervous and worried about his damn proofs, they'd confirmed that she'd come for only one reason: to tie up the loose ends so the atelier could finish printing the run of lithographs the day after Christmas. No wonder she'd been in such an all-fire hurry to get back. No wonder she wouldn't spend another night with him in the country. Mercenary bitch! She was no better than the tramp his old man had run off to Vegas with, that Ruby. He slammed his fist down again, spilling the remains of beef in oyster sauce on the open pages of the glossy magazine.

He gathered up the magazine and the Chinese food and heaved them toward the trash. He'd lost his appetite totally. He was furious. His life had been disrupted

by that damn contract, by his father's visit, by the opening and the holidays. He needed to paint—half-finished
canvases lay all around the high-ceilinged studio. He
opened a beer and paced back and forth the length of
the room, swigging its icy contents occasionally. He
switched on the television, twirled the dial around, and
snapped it off again. He could paint tonight, he supposed, but he wasn't in the mood. Maybe he'd drive up
to Connecticut now and not wait until tomorrow afternoon. He crossed to the window. He'd forgotten about
the snow. Damn!

He turned on the stereo and found his favorite jazz
station. He stretched out on the couch to listen to Billie
Holiday sing. Just what he needed now, he thought bitterly. That VanderPoel woman had really got to him, he
admitted at last. But he could put her out of his mind,
he swore. No woman used Jacques Power—no one! He
hadn't gotten as far as he had without learning all he
needed to know about people and their motivations.
He'd get over her in a little time. He had been doing
fine up to the slip with the kitten. But he was sure she
didn't realize he had brought it to her. Good thing Maroon Garters had answered the door instead of just sitting inside laughing in his white bathrobe while Jacques
Power mooned around in the hall with a cat in a box.
Damn her anyway! Bauman, the guy in the garters,
probably Murdoch too. She and Murdoch were extremely close, anyone with half a brain could see it. He
couldn't keep all the men straight! If she only hadn't
come to the gallery that night. . . . If he only hadn't
touched her again, kissed her soft lips. . . . Smelled the
flowers in her hair and the desire on her breath. . . .

In the large studio, listening to the sad tones of the tragic singer, he looked back on his life. In all those years he had never loved anyone. He had needed his father. Yes, he had needed women too. Many women had sensed the turbulence of his nature and found him more attractive, more of a challenge for it. They had offered themselves to him and he had yielded, willingly. But he had always been disappointed. Thinking back, he saw his life as a slow descent into anesthesia, starting with the day his mother left Patrick and him. Patrick has survived the pain of her desertion through the anesthesia of alcohol. Jacques had survived it by building a wall of insensitivity around himself, a wall constructed of the bricks of mistrust and cynicism. He no longer cared even for himself at times, he thought. That was the source of his lack of feelings for other people.

But he *did* have feelings. Somewhere in his core, a feeling lived and was still growing. He had tried to extinguish it. He had been as brutal and as cruel as he felt capable of being, given the overwhelming physical desire for the woman, a need for her that had shaken him to his core. But it wasn't just sex; sex was available everywhere. It was a need to be with *her*, not with just any woman. He wanted to care for her. He wanted to have her with him at all times. He wanted to know everything about her—how she liked her eggs cooked, what side of the bed she preferred, what her favorite book was. He wanted more days like the morning they had cut down the pine tree. He wanted to go to parties with her and watch her blue eyes appraise the other guests, listen to her opinions always delivered in those gentle, ladylike words that nevertheless left no doubt as to how she felt about their pretentions. He wished he had known her mother; sometimes he wondered how Vanessa would look thirty years from now. Because he wanted to be with her then and have the right to kiss her wrinkled cheek. He wanted to be concerned, to laugh again. He wanted to have children with her.

How could she even contemplate marrying the man he had seen? How could his Scandinavian princess live with a man who wore maroon garters? It wasn't possible. Maybe it was not too late yet. She hadn't even been wearing the ring when she came to see him. Maybe there was still a chance.

He uncurled his long body from the couch and reached for the telephone. He dialed the number burned into his brain. He was aware that the palms of his hands were wet on the plastic receiver.

God, an answering machine. He listened to her soft voice. He hung up without saying anything when the beep indicated he should begin a message. He dialed the number again just to hear her say her name once more.

He tried the number at eleven and again at one before he went to sleep. She was either out late or sleeping at that man's place. This time he recognized the sick thrusts of jealousy that overwhelmed him. How could she? All Jacques had to do was look at her across a crowded room and he could feel the crackling electricity between them. How could she turn her back on that to marry a simp who made a fuss over a two-dollar tip? He laughed out loud in spite of the pain in his chest. Maybe he should get some new clothes. To be taken for a delivery boy twice in five minutes! How Vanessa would love that story. He longed to tell it to her, to watch her clear blue eyes widen in surprise, to know that after a moment's quiet hesitation a giggle would overtake her and the smooth skin beside her eyelashes would crinkle in amusement.

He called the atelier right after nine in the morning and was told that she was on vacation. With *him*, he wondered. On vacation? Or on her honeymoon? Just thinking the word was a torture. Murdoch would know. How could he approach him? Well, if she and Maroon Garters really were an item, Murdoch had been thrown over too. He'd go to him and sound him out, but not at the atelier. Murdoch would tell him— after all, they had something in common. He still had his address around somewhere from the night of the Baumans' party. Where was it? He thought he'd left the scrap of paper in the pocket of the sheepskin jacket.

Chapter Ten

Strains of Debussy came through the door of Maynard's Park Avenue apartment. When he opened the door Jacques saw the look of surprise on the older man's tanned face.

"I was expecting someone else," Maynard said quickly. He wore a dark green silk smoking jacket and perfectly pressed gray slacks.

"I won't keep you long. May I come in just for a minute?" It was easy to be polite when you want something, Jacques thought. Maynard looked around nervously and then stepped back to admit Jacques.

"Ah, Mr. Power. I'm flattered that you'd call on me here, but I'm afraid that I'm involved with someone else. Perhaps if we had met at another time, another place...."

It was Jacques' turn to look surprised. His mouth fell open and he was unable to speak for a moment. So *that's* how it was! But, of course. How stupid of him.

"Don't worry, Murdoch," he said finally. "I'm not here to make a pass at you."

"Oh, well. I'm both relieved and a bit disappointed. Do come in. May I offer you something to drink?"

"Got any beer?"

"My, I'm afraid not. There's little call for beer here. A Scotch perhaps?"

"Fine. Ice and a little water." Jacques sat gingerly on a dainty French antique chair. When Maynard brought him a crystal glass he placed it on an inlaid table in front of him, moving two tiny enamel boxes to make room for the leather coaster.

Maynard settled himself in a matching chair across the table.

"Something wrong at the atelier? I thought we had finished your series. The place hasn't burned down and no one has absconded to Brazil with your plates, although none of that is beyond the realm of possibility."

"Yeah, Bauman walks a fine edge, all right. He's really in to the loan sharks."

"He *is*?" Maynard leaned forward. "Do tell."

"Sure. I looked into his finances before I signed with him. Those prints are time-consuming; I had to be certain I'd be paid whether he sold them or not. So I demanded a big advance and he met all my conditions. You know and I know there's not a bank in town that would lend him that kind of money. He had to get it off the street—that's how desperate he is. Do you have any idea how much he pays to loan sharks a week?"

"No, how much?"

"More than the whole payroll. And that's only interest, remember."

"Oh, poor Richard," said Maynard sadly.

"He borrowed against the probability that my lithos will sell, will make him a lot of money. They will. He's got nothing to worry about."

"That's true. They're the best we've ever done and as curator I see everything."

"He was so nervous things wouldn't go right he sent Mrs. VanderPoel to me as an inducement to finish."

"What?" Maynard asked sharply.

"He offered her to sweeten the pot. I can understand. I don't like doing business like that, but I can see how important it was to him. But that isn't what I came to talk about."

"Just a minute, Power!" Maynard was on his feet in a flash. He dropped his glass on the floor, oblivious when the amber liquid ran over his shoes and soaked into the pastel Aubusson carpet. "Vanessa would never do a thing like that! You conceited pig, you're out of your mind!"

"She did it! How can you deny it?" Jacques rose. This was getting out of hand. He didn't care anymore what she had done in the past. He was here to find out about that other man, about her plans for the future.

"I deny it! I've known her eight years. I know her as well as you know your own mother. She'd never—"

"Maynard, women are all the same," said Jacques with a patronizing sigh of resignation. "They'll do anything for their own ends. You must know that by now. What's in it for her? Are she and Bauman—?"

A searing pain in his mouth brought his words to a quick stop. Jacques fell back into his chair, more in surprise than from the force of the blow. Maynard was agape, staring at his own fist. A trickle of blood began to flow from his hand.

"My God, I *hit* you! I *hit* you. Oh, I am sorry. No, no, I am *not* sorry. How can you say such hateful things about Vanessa? You don't know what you're talking about. I was there when Bauman sent her up to Connecticut. She said you wouldn't want to see *her*, of all people, although, frankly, at the time I got the impression that she was very anxious to see *you*, God knows why. He told her if the proofs weren't back the day after Christmas, we'd all be out of a job, the firm'd go under. If what you're implying were true, he'd have sent some tart like that apparition you brought to the Christmas party. She went because she has no family here, so that no one else's Christmas Eve would be spoiled. She went because Bauman has been good to her over the years and she cares about him. She's an extremely kind and compassionate woman, in case you hadn't noticed, and *you*—you are a first-class bastard!"

Maynard stopped to catch his breath. He pulled a silk handkerchief from his breast pocket and wrapped it cautiously around his hand. A thin smear of blood stained the ecru fabric. "I need an antiseptic. No doubt you've given me rabies. But what a pleasure it was to take a sock at you!" he chortled.

"I don't believe you," said Jacques, wiping blood from his lips with the back of his sleeve. "But it doesn't matter anymore."

"It matters a lot to me. It was an *unmitigated* plea-sure, believe me!"

"I don't mean hitting me. Anyway, you didn't hit me very hard." If Maynard had looked up from his silk-wrapped hand he would have seen Jacques fight-ing the smile that threatened to overtake his lips, de-spite the pain of Maynard's blow.

"Considering that was the first time in my life I ever hit anyone, not bad. I drew blood, didn't I?" crowed Maynard.

"I don't believe you about *her*, but I tell you it doesn't matter. You know exactly what I mean!" he said with exasperation. He wanted to get to the topic of Maroon Garters and here was Maynard prattling on about his pugilistic skills.

"Well, if Vanessa is so easy with her favors, why is she suffering the aftermath so much? I've never seen her so affected by a man," he mused. "She's so dis-traught, she's gone away, you know. I hope she *does* get over you. You're a real brute. Why, I had no idea!"

"She went away to get over *me*? She went away alone? Are you certain?"

"Of course alone. She's not the type who can't go anywhere without a girl friend to shore up her confi-dence. What did you expect? You certainly don't know her very well."

"I know all I need to know. I thought— God, I don't know *what* I was thinking. I had the idea she was going to marry somebody else. I came here to ask you about him. God, Murdoch, where is she?"

"She's gone to Mexico. I don't think I should tell you any more than that."

But Maynard told him.

Vanessa's days and nights fell easily into a pattern of leisure. Each morning she awoke early and watched dawn steal over the bay, the sky changing from gray to shell pink to a brilliant blue. Magenta flowers spilled down the sides of the balcony and contrasted with the cerulean sea. She would brew a cup of coffee and sit on the apartment's balcony in her nightgown and watch while a young whale cavorted in the bay. The whale frolicked and dove, regaining the surface seconds later, its blowhole spewing a wide spray of water in to the still air. One morning a flock of dazzlingly white snow geese flew down the coast, thousands of them catching the gleam of the morning sun on the shining feathers of their wide, white wings. Tears of frustration filled her eyes, a deep sadness at having to experience such a once-in-a-lifetime sight alone, unable to share its unique perfection with anyone.

After coffee she would put on her bathing suit and descend a hundred cobbled steps to the beach on the cove. There she'd swim for half an hour in the quiet water, enjoying the solitude of the early morning hours on the beach. She had discovered on her first full day at Las Hadas that the hotel guests crowded the beach later in the day. She preferred the quiet of the morning, where the only other people were die-hard surf casters escaping the East Coast or Pacific Northwest winter weather. After a swim, she would return to the spacious apartment—it now seemed to be two hundred steps above the beach—shower, and dress in simple sundresses. A newly acquired tan glowed on her cheeks and shoulders.

One day she rented a car and explored Manzanillo, an old fishing town with a surprisingly evident Chinese influence. She learned that the Spanish had traded with the Chinese for hundreds of years throughout the colonial era and that the west coast of Mexico sported a large Oriental population.

Another day she took the car and found a secluded beach five miles north of the hotel. She brought food she had purchased for a picnic in a small grocery store in one of the tiny dust-filled villages near Las Hadas and bought cola drinks throughout the afternoon from a solitary young boy who ran a taco stand under a thatched roof shelter on the beach. She was afraid to try the tacos, but practiced a few words of Spanish with him while she drank the icy soft drinks.

Other days she spent reading at the side of the pool, which was shared by the condominium owners, most of whom were absent like her hosts, the Alba family. At night she ate in the elegant restaurant under the stars on a terrace at the hotel. The sound of waves invisibly lapping the shore a few yards away mixed evocatively with the haunting melodies played by strolling musicians on their violins. She thought the setting under the close tropical stars was like something created from the thin tissue of a young girl's romantic dreams.

No one bothered her and no one spoke to her unless she spoke first. Every guest seemed to have a partner. Even the brown-skinned young girl who came into the apartment each morning to pick up after Vanessa met a young man in the shade of a blooming bougainvillea vine in the late afternoons after the day's work was done. Vanessa passed the pair daily on her way back from the pool and she glanced enviously at the girl, noting the rosy blush on her full, brown cheeks and marveling to hear the high notes of her flirtatious laugh when the young man whispered into her dark, attentive ear. At times Vanessa felt the silence in her own ears grow to a roar, but she told herself that she had come to Las Hadas to heal and that the lonely pain had to be therapeutic—why else would it hurt so?

One late afternoon she left the apartment to take a walk on the beach and admire the sunset before changing for dinner. She decided to walk to the hotel drug store first and chose the path that passed the office instead of her usual direct descent to the beach. She wanted to buy a new paperback book and a handful of postcards.

As she rounded a corner on the twisting, cobbled stairway she caught a glimpse of the fiery red hair of a man just emerging from a taxi. She stopped in her tracks and jumped back into the shadow of the high wall at the side of the stairs. It couldn't be his hair, she reasoned; she was hallucinating, imagining Jacques everywhere she looked. These visions had happened to her before. At Kennedy Airport she had seen the back of a man and she had been utterly convinced the man was Jacques. But when he'd turned, she'd seen a red mustache and goatee and she had realized the man was not more than twenty years old.

But when she dared to draw closer, she knew that

this man *was* Jacques Power. His head was bent in
concentration and he was extracting pesos from his
wallet to pay the driver, but the wild, red hair was
unmistakably Jacques's. With sudden certainty, she
knew she had to get away. She turned and fled back
down the stairs that led to her apartment. She fumbled with the keys until the door at last opened and
she was able to run inside. She slammed the door
soundly behind her.

She waited in the stillness of the empty apartment.
She knew it would be only a matter of minutes until
his knock came at the door. Vanessa had never believed in coincidence and she was under no illusion
that Jacques had simply happened to arrive in Manzanillo. He had followed her here, she knew. She willed
her heart to stop its wild thumping. She held tightly to
the back of a chair to steady the sudden dizziness she
felt.

She whirled around when at last she heard the expected knock on the door.

"What do you want?" She greeted him, an unaccustomed hard edge to her voice.

"Is that any way to say hello? I've just come three
thousand miles or so to see you." The skin at the
sides of his hazel eyes crinkled with quiet amusement
but in their depths she read a nervous glitter.

"Why did you come?" She held tightly to the edge
of the door, afraid that if she let go she might faint.

"Let me in and I'll tell you." He brushed past her
and entered the two-story living room of the luxurious condominium. She smelled his spicy scent as he
passed her and her eyes took in the sight of his tall

frame when he crossed the room to the sliding glass doors that opened to the balcony. She looked greedily at his broad shoulders bulging under the thin fabric of the Indian cotton shirt he wore. A beige linen jacket was flung carelessly over one shoulder. Her senses stirred in his presence, but she vowed that despite his overwhelmingly virile appearance she would hold back now for her own protection.

"When you hide out, you certainly do it in style," he said, turning at last from admiring the view to sweep the room with an appreciative glance. In spite of the pounding in her ears Vanessa's eyes followed the path his eyes took and she saw the decor anew through him. Two oatmeal couches faced each other across a highly polished granite table whose shimmer recalled black Aztec obsidian from the Yucatán jungle. Enormous tropical plants hugged the corners of the room, while a mahogany ceiling fan stirred the air to a gentle breeze. On one wall a gigantic Jasper Johns painting looked down on the minimalist luxury. The seaside wall was constructed entirely of glass. Stretching the entire outside length of the apartment a balcony overlooked the restless ocean, undulating in the slanting late-day sun. In the harbor of Manzanillo a newly arrived cruise ship lay at anchor; strings of Mediterranean lights between its bow and stern already twinkled in the gathering dusk, delineating the craft's sleek lines. The descending sun was well into its nightly floorshow, a stunningly vibrant display of ocher and cerise streaks in the distant clouds. The air had taken on a peculiar golden shimmer.

"Not bad for a working girl, don't you think?" She

looked around the room and laughed nervously. Jacques staring at her, feasting his eyes on her bare tanned legs, on the curve of her breast where it rose above the neckline of the sundress. She wrung her hands together in cold agitation under his intense gaze.

"Am I embarrrassing you?" he asked quietly. "Frankly, I'd forgotten how beautiful you are. You look particularly lovely in this light. A painter always notices the light, you know." His green eyes contemplated her seriously and he took a step toward her.

"The light here *is* magnificent at sunset," she responded. "Like candlelight. It must be atmospheric. I've never seen air that actually had color before." Vanessa knew she was prattling, but she was unable to stop herself.

"I thought you told me you were from Cleveland. The one time I was in Cleveland the air had a distinct color," he joked. "The air was so thick, as a matter of fact, you could cut it with a knife.'

"And odor too. Not quite the same, Jacques. Somehow it lacks ambience when you have to smell the air as well as see it." It felt strange to say his name out loud. It felt strange to be talking to anyone after all the days of silence. Stranger still was the ability to banter with him after all the pain he had put her through. Even as she spoke, she knew her chatty words were nothing but a transparent ploy to buy time.

He moved yet another step closer to her. Although the duplex living room was spacious, Vanessa felt the walls close in on her. She had to do something, the air was electric with tension.

"Would you like a drink?" she asked. "There's some soda. Or I could make you an iced tea."

"Do you have any beer?"

"Not here, but I'll call the office. They'll send a boy down right away with some cold beer." She crossed the room quickly and picked up the telephone. While she ordered the beer she was aware that Jacques had come up behind her. She felt the warmth of his body although he stood far enough away that he was unable to touch her. She felt his eyes on her as if they had a life of their own.

As she hung up the receiver his hands closed on her shoulders and he whispered into her ear, his lips brushing her hair, "Are you afraid of me? Why are you so nervous?" His powerful hands tightened on her shoulders and then slowly rose to caress the skin at the back of her neck. A delicious thrill shot through her body. She remained with her back to him, one hand still resting on the telephone receiver. Her eyes closed and she inhaled deeply.

"Please turn around, Vanessa. I came to see you, not the view of the Pacific Ocean." The strong arms pivoted her body. He held her firmly by the shoulders. One arm, then the other, began a slow, deliberate descent down the silky bare skin of her arms. She was unable to meet his eyes. One look into their hazel depths and she feared the fine edge of control she had been nurturing since he emerged from the taxi would fly out the window. She stared instead at a tiny imperfection in the thread of the cotton shirt. She smelled the delicious scent of him, a heady mixture of sandalwood and heat, the distinct aroma that was Jacques's alone. One hand gently enclosed her waist and deliberately impelled her taut body closer to him; the other firmly lifted her chin so that her eyes would meet his. Still she refused to look at him directly, although she was excruciatingly aware that his lips were closing in on hers.

At last his lips brushed hers gently. At first she willed herself not to react. She stood as still as a marble statue, her eyes closed. His warm lips moved slowly over her eyelids, the tip of her nose, and down to her soft mouth. He kissed her tenderly and then with more determination. He wrapped both wiry arms around her, sculpting her lithe body to his muscular lines, willing her wordlessly to respond. And she did. Quick fires of desire ignited spontaneously within her, burning away all resolve in their roaring flames. Her own arms slipped around his neck and she pulled his head to hers, hungrily kissing him in return. His hands followed the curve of her slim waist and slipped behind her hips, pushing them determinedly against his long thighs. An inadvertent moan escaped her lips when Jacques's mouth moved to the hollow of her slender throat and then to the smooth swell of her breasts above the line of the sundress.

He slipped the strap of the dress off one shoulder, pushing the bodice down and thus freeing one breast. For a short second the cool air kissed her breast before he lowered his warm mouth over the hardening nipple with a satisfied sigh. His tongue circled the nipple slowly, causing a sudden loss of sensation in Vanessa's legs. Her knees buckled beneath her. In one quick motion Jacques lifted her easily and carried her to one of the matching couches, effortlessly opening the zipper of the sundress as he transported her across the room. He lowered her gently to the nubby oatmeal fabric of the sofa. She felt a gentle tug as her dress was removed in an economic gesture to which she did not object. A wild desire coursed unchecked through her limbs as she reached up for him, pulling his length down beside her on the plump upholstery. She began to undo the small white buttons of his shirt, her fingers fumbling with hurry. He whispered in her ear as she worked, his throat ragged with passion, "I need you, Vanessa. Oh, my God, how I need you."

A knock at the door, so gentle and discreet that at first she wasn't certain she had heard it, roused them to their surroundings.

"Damn! Is there no place in this hemisphere where I can be left alone to make love to you?" Jacques rolled to his back.

"It's the beer I ordered for you," she answered, astonished when her words came out in a hoarse whisper.

He sighed in resignation. "Right. I'll take care of it." He looked at her in amusement. She lay in a half daze on the couch, one forearm resting on her fevered forehead, her hardened nipples pointing directly up. A diffused flush colored her neck and breasts. She had to struggle for air and willed her breathing to return to normal. He leaned close to her and whispered playfully, "You look like one of those magnificent odalisques Matisse used to paint when he was young. But perhaps we shouldn't share such a vision of art with the uninitiated help." The knock at the door came again.

Vanessa jumped from the couch in confusion and ran for the door of the master suite.

"What about this?" Jacques called after her. He was one-handedly buttoning his shirt. The other held a rumpled ball of fabric. She looked at him blankly. "Your dress!" he laughed and tossed it to her.

He came into the bedroom a moment later holding two frosty brown bottles of Mexican beer. The bedroom, while spacious, was more intimate in tone than the living room. Silver and bone and warm gray lacquer covered the curved corners of built-in cabinets, which artfully concealed a stereo, a video recorder, and a ticker-tape machine.

Vanessa lay on the bed awaiting him, naked beneath a cashmere throw she'd found folded at its foot.

"We have to talk," he said, sitting on the bed next to her.

"Yes, I know," she answered quietly. "But let's not talk now. Let's make love first and then talk. Talking can wait, but I've been too long without you in my arms. We have lots of time."

"But I have so many things to say," he said in a low voice.

"I know. And so do I, darling." She wasn't afraid of him any longer. She wasn't afraid to call him darling, or any other endearment her heart might burst to say.

"I can't give you what you want, I don't think," he said sadly.

"Why don't you let *me* be the judge of that."

She sat up and put her arms around him, drawing him to her breast. "Let me worry about that." She stroked the wild, red hair at the back of his head, reveling in the stiffness of its wiry texture on her palm.

Jacques undressed and came into the bed next to her. They embraced, tentatively at first. Then he lay back on the pillow and rested one arm behind his head.

"I can't go on. Let me tell you something first."

She propped herself on one elbow to watch the lines of his strong profile. He stared up at the revolving brass ceiling fan, not meeting her eyes.

"I thought you came to me on Christmas Eve just to make certain I'd do the proofs and your firm wouldn't lose the contract. I thought you were using me, just like everyone else. I thought Bauman sent you to me as an inducement...that you and he were— Oh, I can't say it now, it seems so incredible that I could believe that of you." He closed his eyes.

"That's why you wouldn't return my calls?"

"Yes." The whispered word was torn from his depths.

"And that kept you away from me? I had no idea you were so old-fashioned. Why didn't you simply ask me?" she questioned him gently.

"I am not old-fashioned. But I've very wary, I guess. That wouldn't have mattered to me. I could see how you felt about me. Nobody could fake the way you were when we were together."

'So what kept you away?"

"I didn't stay away. I went to your place one night

to tell you that what I suspected didn't matter anymore. God, it sounds so condescending now. I heard some old ladies discussing you in the elevator. They said you were going to marry that ass I saw in your apartment. I was furious!''

"Douglas. That's who you were talking about at the gallery. That's why you were so cruel.''

"Yes.''

"I could never marry an old stick like him. I'd rather be a nun. So what made you change your mind?''

"A gorilla beat some sense into my thick Irish head.'' He smiled at the memory.

"Someone hurt you?'' she asked, alarmed. "*Who* hurt you?''

He pointed to a small swelling on his lower lip, the red crack so tiny she hadn't noticed it before.

"See that? Maynard slugged me.''

"Maynard hit you?'' She asked in disbelief. She sat up quickly. "Maynard hit *you*? Are we talking about the same Maynard?''

"The very same.''

She covered her mouth with a hand to stifle a smile.

"I wish I'd seen that!'' she said at last.

"Can you ever forgive me for the way I've behaved? I'll understand if you can't.'' He looked directly at her for the first time.

"My love, how can you ask? The past is the past. The only time that counts is now.''

"Really?'' His eyes searched hers for some hesitation, some sign that she was holding back on him.

"I don't care, darling. You've come to me now,

have you not? I wouldn't want to experience the pain again, but an easy love is not worth having." She leaned toward his supine form. He reached for her with a long arm.

In the lowering darkness he gathered her body to him with a quiet hunger. When she closed her eyes, he kissed her eyelids slowly, first one then the other. He kissed the tip of her nose. He lowered his mouth to hers and her lips opened beneath the pressure of his to admit his searching tongue. She inhaled the desire-scented fragrance of his breath and sighed with contentment to have him at her side once again. He lowered himself and buried his head in the fullness of her breasts while glowing flames of desire spread like warm oil within her, anointing every inch of her receptive body. His large hands glided lazily over her skin as if he were a sculptor memorizing the lines of a piece of untouched marble before commencing to create a work of art.

He held one rounded breast in his hand and contemplated its shape silently before covering the nipple with his soft lips. She inhaled slowly, trying to hold on to each moment, savoring the ripples of desire that shimmered through her. She twined her fingers in the curls at the back of his head and grasped him firmly to her breast. Her eyes were closed and her lips half parted. The sound of her breath mixed with the muted lap of wavelets on the beach below them. His gestures were slow and dreamlike. Her hands and her head were heavy.

He ran his hand lightly over the mound of her abdomen, tracing above the flesh the ache of desire that throbbed just below it. Her hand was on his back, stroking the skin, wondering that its texture was unlike that of any other's. Like blind people in the gathering darkness they caressed each other's bodies, lingering in the warmest curves, knowing by touch and by the sound of soft gasps which were the tenderest spots, just where the nerves would shiver as the hand found the most secret places.

She uncovered a small scar on his chest and kissed it gently. He spied a spray of freckles on her upper thighs, permanent reminders of an ill-advised sunbath many years before. His fingers traced the path the sun had burned, reluming its own invisible trail in its trajectory. His lips followed his hands, repeating his gentle revelations of the past, enkindling anew in her the joys he had offered for her pleasure once before.

At last, at her whisper of his name, he lowered his body over hers.

They began to make a slow and thoughtful love, a love as quiescent and pacific as the other times had been exuberant. She arched herself closer to him, longing to be as one with him. Her blood simmered with passion as they moved together and she lavished him with the murmured endearments her heart had stored away for him. Feeling braver, more expressive of her feelings than Jacques was of his, she rolled on top of him and covered his hard body with her soft warmth, looking down into his green eyes and telling him with hers that she was his haven, his protection in the world. He was content to let her take the lead, silently allowing her to bring his body to greater flights of sensation and ecstasy. They moved together at her direction, in an easy rhythm that astonished Vanessa who realized she had never before been in a position of such power and control. She moved slowly on his, savoring each sigh and moan of response from his parted mouth.

She buried her head in his neck, covering him with her hair. She listened to the uneven pattern of his breathing, knowing that each gasp was due to a mastery born of an age-old instinct within her and not from any practice. His breath came more quickly now as his blood enriched to the threshold of bursting and she heard her own exhalations join his in harmony of purpose.

Goaded by his appreciative responses, she increased the speed and intensity of her movements against him, fueled to endurance by a source of need for him she had not imagined she possessed, willing at last to recognize that she could not go on in her life without this man at her side. Willing and anxious to give him all of herself, no matter the consequences, to hold back nothing from him in self-protection.

When together they reached the point in their quest where pleasure and desire became all but unendurable, his gentle, long-fingered hands held her head firmly. He pressed his palms tightly to each of her temples so that he looked deeply into her eyes and she into his. She knew he saw the depth of her love for him while he gazed into her soul. And when she felt the tremors shudder through his lean, hard body and heard his moans of release in the still air, she read the love in his eyes, read it as clearly as if he had voiced the words he was incapable of forming. She was filled with an estatic trembling that shook her to the core, blazing within her, increasing to such dizzying intensity that she passed fleetingly into a semiconsciousness that was relieved only by the realization that his mouth had closed once more on hers in a long, hard kiss that served to seal the bond forged between them.

As the embers of the blaze ebbed slowly away she rolled to her side and gathered his spent body to her softness and just held on to him, her arms tightly around his broad back, longing to take his cares on her. She could bear them; she could bear anything as long as he was at her side.

When she awoke the black night was silent. The air was still and as heavy as a velvet shroud. Even without the tick of an internal clock she knew it was late; the usual dissonant strains of mariachi music from the hotel no longer floated past the balcony. She listened to the placid waves lap the sands of the quiet cove that protected Las Hadas from the misnamed Pacific Ocean. When she reached an arm across the bed in the darkness, she was not surprised to find that Jacques was gone.

She rose and put on a peach chiffon dressing gown, an extravagant souvenir of the long-ago lonely trip to Paris. She expected to find him on the balcony. But, determining the entire apartment was empty, although his leather suitcase still lay open in the dressing room off the polished steel and marble master bath, she returned to the balcony and looked out on the soft sands of the cove sharply below. By the light of a setting three-quarter moon she saw a figure hunched on a sea-chiseled rock on the distant beach.

Without bothering to dress or to find shoes, she left the apartment and descended the hundred stone steps to the soft sands of the beach below.

"Jacques, is that you?" She approached the rock where he sat with his back to her. He wore neither shoes nor shirt and he huddled on the smooth rock in only a pair of simple khaki pants. She admired the strong muscles of his back in the shadow cast by the moon. She longed to touch him. She shivered in the cool night air.

"Aren't you cold? Don't you want to come in? I'll make you something warm to drink." She approached the silent form and laid a hand on the skin of his back. She felt him stiffen.

"Jacques?"

"Go away."

Vanessa knew she'd done nothing to bring on this sudden brooding.

"Jacques, don't you want to talk now?"

"No."

"Well, I do and you'll have to listen."

"Go ahead," he said curtly.

"As soon as we get close, you push me away. As soon as I open up to you, you close yourself off like a time-delayed bank vault. You're testing me, don't you think I know that? You're pushing as hard as you can to see how much I can take before I break and run. Well, go ahead, test me! I'm not going anyplace. I love you, Jacques, it's as simple as that. I love *you*—not who you are. Not what you do. Not even what you do for me. When you refused to see me after Christmas, I didn't stop loving you. And if you leave me now, I won't either. You'll have to *throw* me out of your life now—and even then I won't stop loving you."

She came around to the front of the rock and stood with her feet on the wet sand, her back to the sea. She picked up one of his strong, freckled hands from where it rested on his bent knee. She turned it over and kissed the palm. She looked up at him. His hazel eyes were staring down at her with an unreadable expression.

"I'm not your mother, Jacques," she said in a quiet but firm voice. "I'm not going anywhere. I'm going to love you whether you choose to love me or not. I can't help myself—that's just how it is!" She picked up his other hand and held them both to her breasts.

"I know you're afraid. I'm afraid too. I'm afraid that you will fall off a cliff. I'm afraid you'll get run over by a bus. I'm afraid you might get sick and die on me. But I'm not going to hold back anymore because something terrible *might* happen and put an end to everything. Life is too short; it's to be lived, not endured. Pleasure is not the absence of pain—don't you understand?" She squeezed his hands to emphasize her point. "I want too many things that I can't have without you. I'm going to be a living person again. Life is for the living, not the dead. Life is for us! Not for our memories or to dwell on others' past mistakes."

After a long moment in which he said nothing, he

placed his hands firmly on her shoulders. The thrill of his touch went through her.

"You're afraid?" he said in a wondering voice. "You're always so self-contained, so sure of yourself. I never met a woman like you before."

She blinked at his surprising words.

"Me? Sure of myself? No, the only two things I'm certain of are that I'm a fabulous chromist and that I love you—not in that order, either. And sometimes I feel very afraid, especially when you treat me so coldly. I don't even know if you love *me*, but I'm willing to take the chance that you will."

It was so quiet on the beach she thought her ears would burst in the silence while she waited for him to answer her. Even the tiny waves seemed weaker as they splashed on the shore.

At last he said, "I don't know if I love you. I never learned to love anyone, I guess. Maybe I love you but I don't know it's love, could that be?"

"Tell me how you feel," she prompted, her heart flipping over with joy.

"Well . . . well, sometimes I wish there were ten of you, I want to be with you so much. And sometimes I try to imagine what you're going to look like when you get old because I want to be with you then. I want to get old with you at my side." He looked up shyly to see how she was taking what he said.

"I would push your wheelchair over to the easel, if you asked me to," she teased.

"And you could clean my brushes."

"And *you* could clean out the cat's box. She's your cat, isn't she?"

"Yes. Did you suspect?"

"I'd hoped she was." Her heart soared with fullness.

"Vanessa, I'm a man who keeps my word always, you know that, don't you? I never make a commitment I don't intend to keep." The pressure of his hands increased on her shoulders.

She nodded silently at him.

"I promise I won't leave you—unless they carry me out feet first in a box—*that* I cannot help. That's the best I can promise. Is that enough for a start?"

"That's enough for me, my darling." She reached up to grasp his strong hands and pull him off the rock. He wrapped his arms around her waist and she wound hers tightly around his neck, clutching him to her as if to let go would mean the end of the world, their world. Happiness blew off her like gold dust, showering him with her newfound joy. They embraced for a long moment in the predawn stillness.

"I think I'll send Maynard a telegram," she announced when later they walked toward the stone steps that spiraled up to the condominiums. Jacques's strong arm firmly grasped her waist through the diaphanous chiffon whose color unkowingly matched the shell pink of the dawn just breaking behind the rustling palm trees.

"What are you going to say?"

She smiled knowingly. "*I'm* not going to say anything; someone else has already said it better. It's going to read, 'Of all forms of caution, caution in love is probably the most fatal to true happiness.'"

Chapter Eleven

"The first fire of the season," announced Jacques as he dropped the armful of wood he had been carrying in front of the fireplace with a clatter. "I love a fire in the fall." He stacked three logs and lit the fire with a rolled up page from the morning newspaper, standing with his back to Vanessa and watching the hearth until he was certain the kindling had caught. "I don't miss the loft at all."

"You really don't find my place too small?" asked Vanessa, looking up from the needlepoint canvas in her lap.

"With the new studio finished here? No, it's perfect for when we're in town. Or it will be when you're done redecorating." He flopped down on the sofa at her side and stretched his long legs up on the coffee table. He picked up her left hand and idly toyed with the simple gold band on her third finger, turning it around and around absently.

"Do you have to work tomorrow?" he asked her.

"No, not until the next day. Richard's sending out

a job tomorrow night. I still can't get over how accommodating he was when I told him we were moving full-time to Weston."

"Bauman's not stupid," replied Jacques. "It was either make the job fit you or lose the best chromist he'll ever have."

"Do *you* plan to work tomorrow?"

"No. I thought we might take a picnic and drive upstate to look at the leaves changing. Maybe visit some antique shops. What do you think?"

"I'd love it! It's a perfect way to spend the day."

"I don't need to do anything special to have perfect days. Every day is perfect with you, Vanessa," Jacques said in a low voice.

Something in his tone made her turn to look into his hazel eyes. The logs caught and began to crackle, filling the high-ceilinged room with the scent of apples. She felt so serene, so content seated at his side that the nervous glitter that burned in his pupils took her by surprise.

"What's wrong, my sweet? You look upset about something. What's the matter?"

His hand increased its pressure on her fingers.

"Nothing's the matter. I—I just have something to say." He swallowed nervously. "Two things, actually."

"Is it something I've done?" she asked, alarmed. The muscles in her neck tightened at his reply.

"You might say so."

"Jacques, you're torturing me! Tell me."

"You won't laugh at me?"

"I promise," she answered quickly, unable to

imagine what could have agitated her usually self-assured husband so.

"I want us to have a baby," he said in a rush. "That is, if *you* want to," he added just as quickly. A look of relief washed over his freckled face, although the pressure of his fingers, if anything, increased on hers.

A smug little smile played on Vanessa's lips.

"I think that's a wonderful idea," she answered simply.

Jacques did not reply. Instead, he put one arm around her shoulders and kissed her gently on the cheek. He left his lips pressed against her skin. Finally he drew away and emitted a long sigh.

"And the other thing? Is that something I've already done as well?" she asked him.

"You made it happen," he said enigmatically.

"Please tell me before you break my fingers."

Jacques looked down in surprise at Vanessa's left hand crushed in his. Slowly he raised her fingers to his lips and tenderly kissed the tip of each one.

"I love you, you know," he said at last, in a whisper.

She closed her eyes in happiness. "Oh, I know. I've known for a long time. But tell me again," she smiled.

"I'll never stop telling you, my darling." He buried his face in her neck and whispered into the warm skin. "I love you."

Harlequin reaches
into the hearts and minds
of women across America
to bring you

Harlequin American Romance ™·

Enter a uniquely exciting new world with

Harlequin American Romance T.M.

Harlequin American Romances are the first romances to explore today's love relationships. These compelling novels reach into the hearts and minds of women across America... probing the most intimate moments of romance, love and desire.

You'll follow romantic heroines and irresistible men as they boldly face confusing choices. Career first, love later? Love without marriage? Long-distance relationships? All the experiences that make love real are captured in the tender, loving pages of **Harlequin American Romances.**

What makes American women so different when it comes to love? Find out with **Harlequin American Romance!**

Send for your introductory FREE book now!

Get this book FREE!

Mail to:

Harlequin Reader Service

In the U.S.
2504 West Southern Avenue
Tempe, AZ 85282

In Canada
649 Ontario Street
Stratford, Ontario N5A 6W2

YES! I want to be one of the first to discover
Harlequin American Romance. Send me FREE and without
obligation *Twice in a Lifetime.* If you do not hear from me after I
have examined my FREE book, please send me the 4 new
Harlequin American Romances each month as soon as they
come off the presses. I understand that I will be billed only $2.25
for each book (total $9.00). There are no shipping or handling
charges. There is no minimum number of books that I have to
purchase. In fact, I may cancel this arrangement at any time.
Twice in a Lifetime is mine to keep as a FREE gift, even if I do not
buy any additional books.

Name _____ (please print)

Address _____ Apt. no. _____

City _____ State/Prov. _____ Zip/Postal Code _____

Signature (If under 18, parent or guardian must sign.)

This offer is limited to one order per household and not valid to current Harlequin
American Romance subscribers. We reserve the right to exercise discretion in
granting membership. If price changes are necessary, you will be notified.
Offer expires December 31, 1983

AR-SUB-200

154-BPA-NACT

Readers rave about Harlequin American Romance!

"...the best series of modern romances
   I have read...great, exciting, stupendous,
   wonderful."
            –S.E.,* Coweta, Oklahoma

"...they are absolutely fantastic...going to be
   a smash hit and hard to keep on the
   bookshelves."
            –P.D., Easton, Pennsylvania

"The American line is great. I've enjoyed
   every one I've read so far."
            –W.M.K., Lansing, Illinois

"...the best stories I have read in a long
   time."
            –R.H., Northport, New York

*Names available on request.

A Harlequin
ROBERTA LEIGH

A specially designed collection of six exciting love stories by one of the world's favorite romance writers—Roberta Leigh, author of more than 60 bestselling novels!

1 **Love in Store**	4 **The Savage Aristocrat**
2 **Night of Love**	5 **The Facts of Love**
3 **Flower of the Desert**	6 **Too Young to Love**

Available in August wherever paperback books are sold, or available through Harlequin Reader Service. Simply complete and mail the coupon below.

Harlequin Reader Service

In the U.S.
P.O. Box 52040
Phoenix, AZ 85072-9988

In Canada
649 Ontario Street
Stratford, Ontario N5A 6W2

Please send me the following editions of the Harlequin Roberta Leigh Collector's Editions. I am enclosing my check or money order for $1.95 for each copy ordered, plus 75¢ to cover postage and handling.

☐ 1   ☐ 2   ☐ 3   ☐ 4   ☐ 5   ☐ 6

Number of books checked_____ @ $1.95 each = $_____

N.Y. state and Ariz. residents add appropriate sales tax $_____

Postage and handling $_____ .75

TOTAL $_____

I enclose_____

(Please send check or money order. We cannot be responsible for cash sent through the mail.) Price subject to change without notice.

NAME_____
(Please Print)

ADDRESS_____ APT. NO._____

CITY_____

STATE/PROV._____ ZIP/POSTAL CODE_____

Offer expires December 31, 1983   30656000000